The momen with tension . . .

Words. Laura should say something to Alex to make it okay. *No.* Words were not what Alex needed. And they weren't what she needed either.

Alex stood absolutely still as she eased onto her tiptoes and brushed the soft, yielding heat of his lips. Just a touch, not a kiss, really. There had to be a way to express the tenderness she was feeling, and the warmth that was flooding her body now.

"Laura." The word came out strangled. Alex still hadn't moved. But when she pressed herself against him, it was evident that he was aroused.

"Shh." Her mouth found his lips again. This time she trailed her tongue on them delicately and when she pulled away, she saw them glisten with her own touch. This was what Alex wanted, wasn't it? Didn't he know what she craved?

Yes. He read her mind. "Laura," he groaned. Sweeping her into his arms, he headed for the bedroom. . . .

Katherine Kendall says that part of the fun of writing romance novels is the opportunity it provides to indulge her fantasies. While she's already found her fantasy man, *First and Forever* gave her the chance to imagine living an affluent life in New York, complete with a luxury co-op and Jaguar. In reality, Katherine lives a less ostentatious life in Richmond, Virginia, complete with average home and an aging Dodge. Fortunately, as an author of romance novels and children's books, she does have the career of her dreams.

Books by Katherine Kendall

HARLEQUIN TEMPTATION

231–THE MIDAS TOUCH

First and Forever
KATHERINE KENDALL

Harlequin Books

TORONTO • NEW YORK • LONDON
AMSTERDAM • PARIS • SYDNEY • HAMBURG
STOCKHOLM • ATHENS • TOKYO • MILAN

For Lisa Franklin Leach, with love

Published August 1991

ISBN 0-373-25460-1

FIRST AND FOREVER

1

LAURA DANIELS was not—by nature or inclination—a voyeur.

For the most part, she ignored the commanding view afforded by the wall of glass behind her desk. Her office was one of the perks of making vice president. Now that she had it, it didn't seem to matter much. She had better things to do than moon over Manhattan's skyline, breathtaking or not.

Still, there were views, and then there were *views*.

Laura clicked off her desk lamp. The coppery light of sunset filtered into the room, and shadows shimmered on the walls. She removed her glasses and rubbed her eyes. Seventeen floors below her, Sixth Avenue was clotted with rush-hour traffic. But it wasn't the scene on the ground that held her attention.

Directly across the avenue, seventeen floors up, soft yellow light flooded an apartment. In the middle of the room a young man sat at a baby grand piano, hands roaming the keyboard. Laura observed that he was shirtless, clad only in jeans. The scene was so vivid, she could almost hear the sweeping arpeggios as he leaned into the instrument.

Were you considered a Peeping Tom when you just happened to glance out your window and got an eyeful?

Something about life at this altitude made you feel invisible, safe from intruding eyes, Laura thought. At least that was the myth New Yorkers liked to believe. Laura noted a pang of guilt but ignored it. She kicked off her new Italian pumps. They were the most uncomfortable shoes she'd ever had the misfortune to wear, and had put a dent in her checking account that was nearly as hefty as this month's payment on her beloved black Jaguar.

The man at the piano stood abruptly and moved to his window. Arms braced against the sill, he appeared to be surveying the street below. Laura inched her chair closer to her own window. Suddenly he looked up. He was staring straight across at her. Laura was sure of it.

There was no way he could see her; after all, her office was dark. Still, she made a mental note to pull the vertical blinds before she flicked the light back on.

The piano man moved out of view. Laura reached for her lukewarm diet cola and sipped it. She felt vaguely disappointed, as if she'd settled into a darkened movie theatre only to have the reel break after the opening credits.

In the remnants of light she could just make out the hands on her watch: 6:10 p.m. At the rate she was going she'd be here all night. But then, why should tonight be any different?

The piano man reappeared as suddenly as he'd left. Was that a bottle of liquor in his hand? It was hard to say. He stood at the piano, then tilted back his head. Yes, she was sure now: It was a bottle of booze. He was drinking from the bottle.

Laura leaned back, hands laced behind her head. This movie had no subtitles, but the visuals were great. And it beat the hell out of a lot of pretentious foreign films she'd yawned through recently.

She watched as he set the bottle on top of the piano and reached for something. Sheets of paper—music, of course. He crumpled them into a ball, using both his hands. She could see the high arc as he pitched them into the air.

So. Our piano man was a frustrated artist. Or perhaps he was chucking Beethoven across the room, or a beginner's book of scales. No. She liked her first interpretation better.

Again he moved to the window, but this time he sat on the sill, his wide back silhouetted by the light. She was a real sucker for broad shoulders. When it came to male anatomy, nothing could top a muscular back. Tanned, with a soft sheen of perspiration, reflecting the sun . . .

Laura stole a furtive glance at the stack of interoffice memos on the edge of her desk blotter. Yes, they were still there. And they'd be there long after the piano man drew his shades and she returned to earth from this private screening.

He sat motionless. Two apartments away a light flickered on, producing an eerie bluish fluorescence striped by black venetian blinds. But Laura's gaze stayed locked on the dark figure of the piano man, haloed by golden light.

She could picture hands on those shoulders—*her* hands—sweeping down the broad planes of his back. As she trailed her manicured nails down the length of his spine, he would shudder, pulling her closer. She was tall, but he would be taller still, so that when she leaned against him her lips would just graze his shoulder, warm and smooth. . . .

Laura felt her lids grow heavy. Her breathing was quicker than it had been, and she suddenly became aware of her breasts straining against the fabric of her red silk blouse. For comfort's sake she freed a top button, allowing her hand to linger for a moment. Beneath her fingers the soft swell of her breast rose and fell hypnotically. The silk was cool and so impossibly smooth it could have been her own skin she was touching. Her hand traveled leisurely, so slowly that the hard feel of her nipple through her bra and blouse almost came as a surprise....

She could feel him harden against her. She would reach to pull him to her, but he would already be there, finding her mouth before she could tell him what she wanted, for he already knew she was all he'd ever wanted. She was his—

"Slave."

Laura leaped in her chair at the sound of her secretary's voice.

"What?" she barked.

"Was 'twenty-four-hour slave' part of your new job description? You promised you'd be out of here by six sharp—but then you've already heard my lecture on all work and no play."

Rhoda settled heavily into the black leather-and-chrome armchair before Laura's desk. She was seven and a half months pregnant with her first child, but tried to convince anyone who'd listen that it had been more like seven and a half years. "So," she whispered, "who died?"

"I was being . . . contemplative," Laura answered defensively. "You know, you might try knocking sometime."

"I did." Rhoda shrugged. "Guess you were too busy—" she lifted her brows for emphasis—"'contemplating'—whatever that means."

Laura smiled indulgently. Somehow Rhoda managed to pull off a maternal tone, despite being eight years younger. Laura took another sip of cola. "Want something?" she asked. "I just had the fridge restocked."

"Don't mind if I do." Rhoda padded over to the gleaming black cabinet that hid a bar stocked with premium spirits and Baccarat glassware. When she swung open the cabinet door a recessed light flicked on automatically.

Rhoda returned with a bottle of juice. "To contemplation," she said, raising her bottle in a toast as she plopped down. "So anyway, what's bugging you, boss?"

Laura frowned. "Just because you've been reading all those psychobabble books does not mean you have a license to practice psychiatry in the state of New York."

"Just keeping track of symptoms, that's all. Are you conserving electricity, or what?"

"I was just enjoying the view." Laura spun her chair toward the window. Darkness had fallen and the skyline was defined by neon and twinkling lights. In this town, the stars just couldn't compete.

Across the avenue, the piano man had returned to his piano. Good for him.

Rhoda followed Laura's gaze. "Are we discussing the view in general—or that view in particular?"

"Where?" Laura stalled, feeling strangely proprietary.

"The half-naked hunk across the street." Rhoda pointed. "Or hadn't you noticed?"

"'Hunk'?" Laura's voice moved up the scale half an octave. "What hunk?"

"Yeah, right," Rhoda scoffed. "I suppose you were staring at the Queensborough Bridge."

Laura nodded. "In all its glory."

"You're a rotten liar."

"I resent that," Laura objected. "I'm a great liar. I minored in lying in college."

"And majored in men?"

"Those days are long past, my dear. Need I remind you that I am rapidly approaching my middle years?"

"Give me a break," Rhoda snorted. "Thirty-five is not exactly retirement age. Besides, you look twenty-five."

"I knew there was a reason I got you that raise."

"No, I'm serious. I'd pay big money to be tall, blond and blue-eyed. Hell, I'd pay big money to be able to see my own feet right now. They *are* still there, aren't they?" She peered over her knees as best she could, her round face momentarily obscured by a curtain of dark curls.

"Looks good, so far."

"Size tens and I care barely see 'em." Rhoda pushed her hair off her face. "Seriously, now. You're not having the birthday blues, are you?"

"No. My birthday's not for a month. This is just a warm-up drill." Laura gave a self-deprecating laugh. "People tell me I look younger than my age, but I'm the only one who knows how much harder I have to try. There's the sunscreen to prevent new wrinkles, the moisture cream to get rid of the ones I already have, the frosting to hide my gray hairs, the needless aerobics to convince my fanny to defy gravity... What's next? Tummy tucks and liposuction?"

Rhoda shook her head, her expression grave. "A nursing home in Miami. How's your shuffleboard?"

"I'm serious, Rhoda."

"So am I. Laura, you're in the prime of your life."

"Tell that to my gynecologist."

"Oh, yes—" Rhoda nodded "—the ol' biological time clock."

"More like biological time bomb, in my case. Last time I saw her she asked if I saw children in my future. I had to tell her I wasn't even sure I saw *dating* in my future."

"But you're not the only woman in this city with this problem," Rhoda reassured her. "And at least you're doing something about it, taking the reins."

Laura sighed heavily. "The Great Hubby Hunt."

"Laura Daniels stalks Big Game," Rhoda added, giggling.

"On the streets of Manhattan, no less. Tells you something about my chances, doesn't it? In any case—" she rubbed her chin thoughtfully "—I can't sit around forever, waiting for fate or Cupid or whoever's in charge of these things. I've got to take control of my destiny. Although I must admit I never dreamed I'd be desperate enough to resort to a matchmaker."

"You mean 'personal introduction consultant,'" Rhoda corrected, in an affected Upper East Side accent.

"Yeah, and a sanitation engineer still picks up garbage. A rose is a rose, kiddo."

"Well, if it works it'll be worth the trouble."

"And expense?"

"You can't put a price on love, Laura."

"How's five grand grab you?"

Rhoda's jaw dropped in disbelief. "Boy, am I in the wrong line of work."

"That's a lot of nights in a singles bar," Laura quipped. "I'm beginning to have serious doubts about this 'investment.'"

"Hey, it worked for Larry, didn't it?" Larry Porter was Laura's boss. He'd found his third wife, Ginger, using the same matchmaker.

"I don't know about that." Laura tried to suppress a smirk. "I've got dust bunnies under my bed with higher IQs than Ginger."

They laughed, then settled into silence. Across the way, the piano man was still playing.

"You know," Rhoda said quietly, "I know who he is."

"Who?"

"The reason you have the lights turned off."

"The reason I have the lights turned off—"

"Is to get a better look at that bod."

"Rhoda. You're so . . . crass."

"Because I'm right?" she teased.

Laura ignored her, taking a sip of her cola. She wasn't about to press for details. Rhoda would get around to it in her own sweet time.

"I've seen him at Greene's deli," she admitted. "We were in line together one day. He warned me not to order the corned beef, and we got to chatting. He mentioned he lived upstairs from the deli."

"Oh, Rhoda—" Laura eyed her skeptically "—how can you possibly tell it's the same guy?"

Rhoda struggled up out of her chair and peered out the window. "It's him," she pronounced. She twisted around to wink at Laura. "A woman knows these things."

"The shoulders," Laura stated matter-of-factly.

"Yep," Rhoda confirmed. "And if you like 'em this way, you ought to see them up close and personal. Or, we could just dig up a good pair of binoculars."

"Rhoda! Men are not *mere* sex objects. They're *human beings*, with feelings and needs," Laura scolded jokingly.

"Not at this distance, they're not."

Laura laughed, but watching the piano man rhythmically sway to his music, she wasn't so sure Rhoda was right. Reluctantly she turned on her desk lamp, and the images outside were blotted out by the light.

AROUND ELEVEN O'CLOCK Laura decided to call it quits. She turned off the lights and took one last look across the avenue.

The piano man's apartment was dark.

It was just as well. Fantasy, unfortunately, was always better than reality.

BY SEVEN the next morning Laura was back at the office, poring over a presentation for a new client, a manufacturer of disposable diapers. Breakfast consisted of a jelly doughnut and several cups of strong black coffee. By noon she was famished.

What she needed was some protein to see her through the afternoon. Something substantial. Pastrami, maybe. Or corned beef. Corned beef on rye. The very thought made her mouth water.

But Rhoda, who usually picked up lunch for the office, was in the middle of a sixty-page memo on her word processor. She'd also been complaining all morning that her feet were swollen. The least Laura could do was volunteer to get lunch. Besides, she could use the fresh air.

Laura grabbed her purse and coat and headed for the front office. "I'm getting lunch today," she announced to Rhoda.

"*You?*"

"Yes, me," Laura responded belligerently. "You have a problem with that?"

"Not *me*," Rhoda assured her quickly. "Here—" she handed Laura a small memo pad "—I use this to take orders. Where are you going?"

"Oh, I dunno," Laura hedged. "The deli, maybe. I had this sudden craving for a corned beef on rye."

"Greene's, huh?" Rhoda smirked, eyeing her boss carefully as she passed the notepad around the room. "If memory serves, you had the same craving last night."

"You know, that raise hasn't been finalized yet, Rhoda," Laura gibed. "Can't a woman get a bite to eat without getting the third degree?"

"Of course," Rhoda said with exaggerated seriousness. "We all get strange cravings now and then. And Laura—"

Laura turned at the doorway. "Yes?"

"Be sure to check out the special on tenderloin—"

Laura didn't wait to hear the rest.

THE DELI WAS PACKED. Just taking a number to be served proved a logistical challenge. Laura stood in line, pressed against the long glass display case. Behind it a half-dozen employees clad in once-white aprons scurried purposefully, trading good-natured insults with the customers. A long row of red leather booths lined the other half of the deli, and a few Formica tables were squeezed into the front section. Every seat was taken.

Laura surveyed the room without quite knowing what she was looking for. Now that she was here, she couldn't imagine why this had seemed like a good idea. Something about fresh air, wasn't it? In fact she was stifling in her peach cowl-necked sweater dress. She brushed back a few damp strands of hair from her forehead, and pictured her mascara puddling as the minutes ticked by.

"Honey. Whaddya want, an engraved invitation?"

"Oh—sorry," Laura murmured, checking her number stub. "Number eighty-seven?"

"Not for much longer."

"I need—" she dug into her purse for the list "—well, here. This'd probably be easier."

"Easier?" demanded the man behind the counter. He rolled his eyes heavenward. "Easier is a condo in Miami Beach." He glanced over her notes. "German bologna on white? Where are you from? Iowa?"

"Hey, I'm just the go-between," Laura protested.

"Don't worry, honey, I gotcha covered."

He leaped into action and Laura stepped back away from the counter. The noise was deafening—dishes clattering, employees yelling.

She should have had something delivered. This was a waste of valuable time. Based on the most intangible desire, she was doomed to spend half her day melting away here in a scene from Dante's "Inferno."

Then she saw it: his back. In the very last booth, hunched over a spread-out newspaper. He had a black rib-knit sweater on, with a white oxford-cloth shirt underneath. Thick blond hair grazed his collar—definitely longer than was fashionable.

Laura felt her heart do gymnastics. Her cheeks, already flushed, grew hotter. She felt the way she had in seventh grade, spying on Brad whatever-his-name-was in the lunchroom of Kennedy Junior High. Brad had had nice shoulders, too, she recalled. Some tastes evidently developed early.

Her line of sight was momentarily blocked by a large man wearing a beret. When he moved on, she could see again the object of last night's fantasy. He reached for his cup of coffee and gulped it down, but his gaze continued to rest on the newspaper. He was alone in the booth.

Her pulse was hammering away in her throat—as if she cared; as if this silly game *meant* anything. Still, she'd gone this far. She felt compelled to finish what she'd started.

The mission was clear: She had to get a look at his face.

Why, she couldn't say. Hers was not to reason why. Hers was to do it and then hightail it out of there before inflicting any further indignity on herself. *And* she *was turning thirty-five in a couple of weeks?*

Easing through the crowds jamming the aisle, Laura moved closer. From ten feet away, he looked at least as good as he had from the front of the deli. She paused, pretending to check her watch.

She was so close she could reach out and touch him. She almost turned away, but then the piano man stretched, lacing his fingers together overhead. No wedding ring, she noticed, pleased with her spylike acuity. No watch either, which confirmed, along with the hair and clothing, that he was certainly not one of her fellow Madison Avenue types. Ad executives even made love with their watches on. At least, she did!

Laura turned away from her prey, casually inspecting the counter. On the wall at the far end of the room was a poster of a cow, split into its edible parts and labeled Tenderloin and Shank. Laura leaned over the display case, pretending to study its contents, a collection of unidentifiable, fleshy lumps that looked like grayish Play-Doh. All of them were wreathed in kale. The sight made her feel vaguely nauseous, but she held her ground. All she had to do now was execute a casual turn and—

"How many, dear?" It was a petite woman, probably Mrs. Greene, peeking over the display case.

"Oh, uh...I don't know," Laura stalled.

"Let me get you a little piece. You decide, then. All right?"

"Well, now, um, that depends on what it is." Laura smiled ingratiatingly.

"What it is? She wants to know what it is?" Mrs. Greene looked up as though seeking divine intercession.

"Tongue."

The voice coming from behind her caught Laura completely off guard. She spun around and saw him looking up at her, still seated before his newspaper.

The face was devastating. To die for. Stunningly handsome.

It was also about fifteen years her junior.

"It's beef tongue. For sandwiches. You know." He smiled.

"Oh," Laura managed. "I've uh, never seen it...entire, like that."

The man—the *young* man—nodded.

"Deli food always treads the fine line between delicious and disgusting. Sometimes it's best not to see things till they're safely between a couple of pieces of rye bread."

Laura had no idea how to respond. She was stunned into silence. *This* was the piano man? She had been lusting after a veritable teenager? Sneaking around spying on him like some depraved cradle-robber?

Rhoda. Rhoda *knew*. She'd seen him already, and had gone right ahead and set Laura up for this debacle. Tenderloin, indeed!

"Not a big deli fan, I guess," he observed.

"Uh, I usually send my secretary to pick up lunch." *My ex-secretary,* she added to herself.

"Secretary, huh?" He looked her over, nodding slightly as though considering that bit of information, then grinned. "Executive type, I see."

Laura stood there, her mind blank, staring into two appraising green eyes. Two *young* green eyes, she reminded herself, but too late. Despite her better judgment, she could feel her resistance melting.

His features were hard-edged: strong chin, Roman nose, full, sculpted lips. It was a confident face; still,

something about it advertised that it was mainly the
confidence of youth. There wasn't a laugh line to be seen,
but it was more than that—something intangible. Maybe
the way his smile curved down at the corners a bit—a
smile that reminded her of that secret certainty that
you're going to own the entire world someday soon. The
feeling you take for granted at nineteen and ache for by
twenty-nine.

And yet, there was also in those eyes a hint of something older—something melancholy. A memory, perhaps. She couldn't meet his gaze.

"Eighty-seven. Pickup for eighty-seven!"

"Oh, that's me," Laura said, breaking his spell. "I have
an order up."

"Hmm." He nodded, looking down and toying with
the edge of his paper. "If you need a place to sit—"

"No, that's okay. I—"

"I mean, I'm leaving soon."

They were stepping all over each other's words. She
felt as if she'd entered some sort of time warp since she'd
set foot in Greene's, regressing into adolescence. Of
course, when she was younger, guys didn't look like this.

"Really, I don't mind." He looked up at her and smiled
again, leaving her dazzled.

"Well, okay. For a second. I'll just get my order."

Was she out of her mind? She had work to do—
mountains of it. Half of her office was starving to death
while she was carrying on her little dalliance with someone young enough to be—well, her brother. She'd con-
cede that much anyway.

She reached the register and paid the clerk. Picking up
the bag of sandwiches, she stole a glance at her table-
mate-to-be. She thought of those booths at fairs and

carnivals where they tried to guess your age. She'd never been particularly good at pinpointing ages.

He could be twenty. Then again, he could be a well-preserved, say, twenty-five.

Where was she at age twenty-five? Grad school, Columbia University. And at twenty-one? Drinking her first legal glass of wine somewhere. Wearing a dress size in the single digits. Backpacking in Europe after graduating from college, playing the bohemian.

And what was she playing now? Big sister?

Lord, she'd been young back then.

She took her change and dropped it into her purse. There was a tube of Retin-A wrinkle cream in the bottom. She'd just had her prescription refilled yesterday.

Lord, did she feel old!

If she darted out the door quickly, she could sneak back to the office and no one would be any the wiser. Except Rhoda, who would naturally have to be murdered.

She was still debating the options when she heard his voice, penetratingly musical in the din.

"Here, let me give you a hand with that."

He looked so sincere—so utterly without pretense in a city founded on it—that she couldn't resist.

Without a word of protest she handed him the bag and followed him back to the booth. As she settled onto the red leatherette, she wondered how on earth she was going to explain all this to her starving staff. One thing was certain: From now on, she'd be safe from lunch duty.

He reached across the table and shook her hand firmly. "Alex Shaw."

"Laura Daniels."

"You have a hearty appetite, Laura Daniels."

"Well—" she returned his smile "—I'm eating for five."

"Oh?" he raised his brows.

"My co-workers across the street."

"And I'm holding you up."

"That's okay. Let them eat cake."

A chubby young waitress appeared with a glass coffeepot and refilled Alex's cup.

"Thanks, Jan," he said. "Bring me another bagel when you're back this way again, will you?"

"Sure." The waitress nodded, turning to Laura. "Coffee?"

"I suppose," Laura answered. "Why not?" *Why not, indeed?* She could think of a few hundred good reasons why not.

The waitress flipped over Laura's cup and filled it. "Wanna menu?"

"No, I'm just—" She wasn't sure *what* she was doing.

"Passing through?" Alex offered.

"Whatever." The waitress shrugged, spinning on her heel.

"I love New Yorkers—" Alex chuckled "—they're always so polite and deferential."

"So you're not a native, and yet you know beef tongue when you see it. Where are you from?" Laura asked.

"Maryland. Home of dynamite crab cakes and dynamite baseball."

"Well, crabs I would recognize, but don't let a Yankees fan hear you talking publicly about the Orioles like that."

"Don't worry, I don't want to start a riot." Alex laughed. "And what about you? You don't sound like a New Yorker."

"How's a New Yorker supposed to sound?" Laura countered.

"Like the letter *r* hasn't been invented yet."

"Actually, I hail from Connecticut," she said, doing her best Yalie imitation, an updated Katharine Hepburn. "We use *r*s, but sparingly. To tell the truth, though—" she leaned a little closer "—I claim to be a native. It has a certain cachet I like."

"Your secret's safe with me."

Laura found herself smiling again. This time she wasn't afraid to look into his eyes. "You know, I've seen you around, I think," she admitted, surprising herself.

"Yeah?" His eyes narrowed. "Then how come I've never seen you?"

Because I'm a Peeping Tom, Laura thought, but said: "I try to keep a low profile."

"Oh, really?" He propped his elbow on the table and cupped his chin in his hand. "So, let me guess: What does Laura Daniels do for a living?"

"I'm with Tate and O'Neill. A corporate VP." She noticed her voice rising slightly with pride. Boy, how she'd busted her tail to get there.

"The ad guys?" he asked with surprise.

"Yep. That's what it says on my business cards—'the ad guys'!" She sipped her coffee.

He ignored the joke. "You mean—" he leaned toward her, eyeing her quizzically "—the people who gave the world 'Yum-Yums—the gum-gum when your tum-tum's been dumb-dumb'?"

He sang the jingle in such a nasal singsong that it was all Laura could do to stifle a laugh. Still, the Yum-Yum account had been her baby. And while the lyrics were not exactly Tony-award-winning material, they'd served their purpose well enough.

"As a matter of fact—" she cleared her throat "—I was account coordinator for that campaign."

"Naw." Alex leaned back against the seat, his arms crossed over his chest. He had a tantalizing dusting of dark blond chest hair at the V of his sweater. Laura tried not to stare at it. *"You?"*

"Who'd you expect?"

"I don't know." He shrugged. "Some little bald guy from Jersey in a plaid polyester jacket."

"Advertising is a very lucrative business, I'll have you know," Laura shot back.

"Yeah, I can tell." He nodded at her lady's Rolex watch. "What's the going rate on souls these days?"

"You're suggesting I've sold out?" Laura inquired icily.

"Worse. You sold Yum-Yums."

"As it happens, their sales shot up forty-two percent the first quarter after our campaign was launched."

Alex shook his head and brushed back a lock of blond hair from his forehead. "Just what the world needs. An antacid you can blow bubbles with."

"It fills a niche in the market." Laura tore at her napkin in silence while the waitress delivered Alex's bagel.

"What niche?" he demanded. "All those six-year-old ulcer patients out there?" His look was challenging.

Boy, were her instincts fallible when it came to men. What was she doing here, subjecting herself to a lecture on advertising from some arrogant postpubescent piano player? What did *he* know?

"What do you know, anyway?" she countered.

"I know I could write a better jingle." He shook his head. "Do you have any idea how many times I've been tooling along nicely, minding my own business, when suddenly out of nowhere that obnoxious Yum-Yum jingle enters my head? It's like being invaded by some alien presence. I once hummed it for three hours straight and seriously considered consulting an exorcist."

"Exactly!" Laura pounded the table with the flat of her hand for emphasis. "That's the genius of a classic jingle. Good or bad, it stays with you. Sure, it may be with you in the car, or the shower, but as long as it's with you when you push that shopping cart down row 4-A where the antacids are located, we've done our job. It doesn't have to be Bach. In fact, studies show it's the annoying jingles that are often the most effective." *There!* She felt better.

"Well, then, the Yum-Yums song is destined to become a classic."

"At least we've found a point of agreement." Laura reached for her bag. "Now, if you'll excuse me, I have pastrami to deliver." She stood. "I must get back to plying my dirty little trade."

"Wait." Alex stood, too. He was a good six feet two — easily half a foot taller than she was. Slender, if solidly built. He touched her shoulder, then pulled his hand away self-consciously.

"Don't take this personally, okay?" he ventured. "I just don't see why they have to be so, you know, obnoxious."

"Strange," Laura grated. "I was going to ask the same thing about you."

"Touché." Alex laughed, not the least bit unnerved. "All I mean is, why can't it be more interesting, more lyrical?"

"Everyone's a critic." Laura sighed. "Tell you what — get your degree, get your feet wet struggling in the business for a few years. Then we'll talk. As it stands, you couldn't sell a—" she glanced at their table "—a bagel to a starving man."

Good work, Laura, she chastised herself. Well, the guy was unsettling her — something even the most irate client could rarely do. One minute he was so cocky she

wanted to scream; the next, so vulnerable she wanted
to . . . Well, she wasn't sure what she wanted.

She looked up to see Alex holding a bagel half,
smothered in cream cheese, in his right hand, a half-
moon bite missing. He took a small, theatrical bow.
"Ladies and gentlemen," he intoned, "an ode to the
humble bagel."

Laura's eyes darted around the deli. She was clearly in
the company of a complete lunatic—not an uncommon
occurrence in New York, but one she generally tried to
avoid unless the loon was a close personal friend.

As she looked on with a mixture of awe and embarrassment, Alex began to sing in a perfect, clear tenor:

Ask all the greats,
From Kant to Hegel,
They all prefer
The humble bagel.
It's not what it is,
It's what it's not;
Without that hole,
You'd lose a lot—

"That's okay—" Laura held up her hand "—I get the
drift."

Alex acknowledged the smattering of applause.
"Bravo!" shouted an elderly couple standing near the
counter.

Laura shook her head in utter amazement. The tune
was playful and wistful. And absolutely wrong for a
thirty-second food spot.

"Well," Laura conceded, "not bad for your first time
out. You may have a future writing music for off, off, off

Broadway. But you made me want to love the bagel, not eat it."

"Hunger takes many forms," he pronounced seriously.

"In any case—" Laura cleared her throat "—thanks for the show. I have to go grease the wheels of capitalism."

"More Yum-Yums?"

"Kitti Bran, actually."

"Which is?"

Laura sighed. "High-fiber cat food." She moved to leave.

"Constipated cats the world over will sing your praises," he remarked, following her.

"Long before you catch anyone singing 'Ode to a Bagel,'" she muttered, finally reaching the door.

WHEN SHE RETURNED to the office, Laura ignored the complaints of her hungry co-workers and stalked over to Rhoda's desk.

"Too young?" Rhoda inquired, refusing to look up from her typing.

"Actually, no," Laura retorted. "Too obnoxious."

"And what about the shoulders?"

"Rare." Laura sighed. "Way too rare."

2

"BOY OR GIRL?"

Laura looked up at the Bloomingdale's saleslady impatiently tapping one of her sensible-but-tasteful shoes on the carpet.

"Now, how would I know? Give me one in pink and one in blue." Actually, Laura had bet a large sum in the office pool that Rhoda would have a girl, so if her secretary knew what was good for her, she'd come through.

Either way, Laura thought, *I may end up being just about the first person to know.* In a foolish moment Laura had agreed to be Rhoda's Lamaze partner, since there was every chance that Rhoda's Marine husband would still be stuck on patrol in the Mediterranean by delivery day. Since then, Laura had become more and more involved in the seemingly endless saga of the pregnancy. This was not the first time she'd found herself in the infants' section instead of prowling the Donna Karan's where she belonged.

She had run into Bloomie's looking for something to wear to her dreaded meeting with the matchmaker, and had ended up buying tiny stretch-terry cloth jumpsuits instead.

The *match*maker! The very word conjured up Yenta the matchmaker from *Fiddler on the Roof.*

Laura began unconsciously humming "Matchmaker, matchmaker . . ." under her breath, till she noticed the saleslady giving her sidelong glances. *Well,* she chided herself sarcastically, *if I could find a good man who was single to boot, I wouldn't be going to a matchmaker, would I?*

Maybe not, although it was Larry who had convinced her to try Margo Morgenroth on the strength of his own alleged success in meeting and marrying Ginger.

Some recommendation!

Still, on her own she hadn't done so well. Take Gerald, her former "significant other," for example. In the two years they'd lived together, he'd degenerated from being her knight in shining armor to a tedious hypochondriac with a compulsion for student nurses. After throwing him out, she was certain she could soon do better. Since then, however, the only man she'd met who was neither married nor gay, had been that overgrown adolescent from the deli.

She picked up a stuffed bear wearing a pin-striped suit and squeezed it. She had a meeting to prepare for and here she was wasting time, buying baby clothes and reliving, for the nineteenth time in the past three days, her run-in with Alex Shaw. The things she should have said!

Well, you always thought of the good put-downs when it was too late.

Laura found herself humming again. Then she realized what it was she was humming. Damn him! She couldn't get that blasted "bagel" song out of her mind. It crept up on her in the shower and in the elevator. It was like . . . like being taken over by an alien presence!

"Stop it," she said aloud.

"Pardon me?" the saleswoman asked coolly.

"Nothing," she replied, more curtly than intended. "Just wrap up my purchase."

"Yes, ma'am."

Laura felt badly, as always, when her notoriously sharp tongue got out of control, but a moment later any regret was wiped away.

"Is it your daughter who is having the baby?" the woman asked with exaggerated sweetness.

"My what? My daughter?" She was about to explain to the woman that it would be physically impossible for her to have a daughter of childbearing age, but some cruel part of her mind had done the math while she formulated a tart response. No, it wasn't impossible at all. She took a deep breath, picked up her package and simply said, "Touché."

"Yes, ma'am." The saleslady smiled triumphantly.

LUTÈCE WAS LOCATED in a lovely old brownstone. It had an oddly homey appearance for one of New York's most expensive and exclusive restaurants. The importance of the Universal account to Tate and O'Neill was clearly signaled by the fact that her boss Larry Porter scheduled the meeting here. It was intended as a message to Howard Gordy, head of Universal Foods, that their firm would treat him with all the respect and deference they could muster.

Or all the respect they could fake. Howard Gordy was infamous as a royal pain in the ass, and worse when, as now, he was into his third martini. But his account would be worth tens of millions of dollars.

Across the table, Larry gave her a discreet wink. Laura suppressed a smile. After working together for a number of years, she and Larry read each other's minds easily.

Larry was a big, jowly man in his fifties with a receding patch of pure white hair. He came from the hearty pat-on-the-back school. With Laura he was unfailingly paternal, but she'd been well rewarded for her expertise in handling major clients, and for the most part she liked him. She didn't exactly trust him, but she did like him. To the extent that he was a schemer and a manipulator, at least he was a transparent one.

As for Gordy, he was even shorter than she remembered from their previous meeting—five feet four inches, giving him every benefit of the doubt and full credit for his thick-heeled cowboy boots, which were made of some hideous reptilian skin. He had a little round head that reminded her of an acorn squash, protruding ears, and black hair slicked back with Brylcream. From all appearances, he and Larry seemed to be getting on famously. That was one of Larry's great skills—the ability to cozy up to money with sincerity.

Gordy, who hailed from Austin, Texas, owned the controlling interest in Universal Foods, one of the largest diversified food manufacturers in the world. Half the food in Laura's refrigerator, from frozen yogurt to baby dills, consisted of Universal products, although they were marketed under various different labels. Now Gordy was looking for a new ad agency to make Universal a household word. The top five agencies in New York were all romancing him, but as far as she knew, Tate and O'Neill still had as good a shot as any.

Larry gave Laura a look that signaled to her that the period of small talk was over and that business should commence.

"We've got some truly innovative concepts on-line for Universal," Laura began.

"We're gonna knock your socks off, Howard," Larry chimed in. "Laura here's our brightest star at Tate and O'Neill. She handled the Sentinel Communications account. Let's see . . . Yum-Yums, Diaper Time, Southeast

Air . . . and of course you remember the Taco King campaign with the talking taco?"

"That was your baby?" Gordy asked Laura.

Laura nodded proudly. That campaign had taken a foundering chain and turned it around virtually overnight. She'd opted for humor over hard sell in the thirty-second spots—against the opinions of just about everyone at the firm—and it had paid off big.

Gordy slugged down the last of his martini. "Boy, I loved those ads. Had me rolling on the floor every time they came on." He leaned forward in his chair, pushing aside his table setting.

"Yep. Good for tacos, but not for me. Let me tell you what I have in mind. Then you can tell me if you can do it or not." Gordy didn't sound as though he were anticipating any disagreement.

Oh, no! Laura thought, catching Larry's eye. They were about to enter the Twilight Zone. Clients' ideas were seldom helpful. That's why ad agencies were invented.

"I want something to tie all our many products together. A kind of a look . . . a kind of a feel . . ." He held out his arms and made a little arc. "I'm thinking in terms of a unifying musical and visual theme. Like McDonald's with all that hazy gold light and the tune that changes from commercial to commercial but is basically always the same. You know what I mean—a tune, a song, whatever you call it, that will represent my no-wax floor and my lo-cal corn dog with equal—" he paused "—majesty."

Laura barely contained herself from rolling her eyes. This was nothing at all like the ideas they had worked up, and Gordy wanted to make a final decision within two weeks. The kind of campaign he was talking about took extraordinary planning—work that they could not possibly get done before the deadline.

Just like Gordy to throw a monkey wrench like this into the works at the last minute. A single musical theme to be used in commercials for everything from frozen pizza to cat food? It was ridiculous and impossible.

Laura glanced over at Larry for support, but his eyes had a glazed look. *Terrific!* The mention of McDonald's, the biggest single advertising account in the world, had given Larry visions—not of mere tens of millions, but hundreds of millions.

"Well, Mr. Gordy," Laura began, "that would be a fine idea, but—"

"It's a great idea, Howard," Larry interrupted, snapping out of his trance. "We could take that ball and really run with it."

Laura squeezed a lime into her sparkling water. "Perhaps," she added calmly, "we should dribble the ball a bit first, if I may mix my sports metaphors." She turned her full attention to Gordy, making direct eye contact with him to indicate that she now had the reins. "You're talking about a series of completely different ads, for completely different products, all aimed at different groups of consumers, all using the same musical theme?"

"Well . . ." Gordy pursed his lips. "Variations on a theme, maybe. You know—one jazzy, one classical, one rock and roll."

Laura smiled bleakly. Conversations like this made her regret her promotion.

"May I take your order now?"

Larry and Laura sighed audibly. Saved by the waiter.

Lunch at Lutèce was prix fixe, which meant that they had only three choices. There was a poached salmon, a tornedos of beef, and veal sweetbreads. Sweetbreads

were a bit like beef tongue—something you could eat
only if you didn't think about it too much. What was it
Alex had said? "They tread the fine line between disgusting and delicious"? Yes, that was it. Like the "piano
man" himself.

Now, why hadn't she come up with that line when it
would have done some good?

"I'll have the salmon," Laura said distractedly, continuing to look over the menu description of the dish
without really reading it. Sweetbreads, right. Tell people what they are and you wouldn't sell many. Talk about
an advertising challenge. Maybe Alex would like to
compose a little ditty for *them,* but of course he wouldn't
find any easy little rhymes like *bagel* and *Hegel,* which,
if you thought about it, was a pretty lousy combination. Bagels and German philosophers?

"There!" Gordy pounded his fist on the table, making
the glassware rattle.

"'There' what?" Laura inquired anxiously, tossing
down her menu. "What's wrong?"

"Wrong, my dear? What's right, you should ask."
Gordy turned to Larry. "Damned if you weren't kidding
about her, Porter. This girl doesn't waste any time."

Mother told me there'd be days like this. What did he
have in mind now?

Larry smiled politely. "I don't quite follow—"

"That tune, Porter, that tune. Hum it again darlin'."
Gordy nodded encouragement at Laura.

"Hum what?" Laura frowned. Had she been . . . Oh,
no! What an embarrassing habit. She was really going
to have to watch that. She'd been humming the piano
man's bagel song.

"Sorry, gentlemen. It's a bad habit of mine, when I'm reading or thinking. Sorry for the interruption." Laura smiled apologetically.

"Sorry, hell," Gordy said. "That's just the kind of thing I was looking for."

"But that's not really—" Laura began, but Larry had sensed an opening and moved quickly to capitalize on it.

"That's all right, Laura," he interjected smoothly, signaling her to keep quiet. "You see, Howard, that tune Laura was humming was just written by one of our people for another client, but if you like it . . ." He let the implication hang.

"I like it," Gordy answered forcefully. "But you'll have to decide whether I get it, or your other client gets it. Your call, Porter. Now—" he pushed back his chair and stood "—I have to go to the cowboys' room."

He strutted off. Laura toyed with the lime in her spring water. Larry fiddled with his fork.

A few seconds passed before Laura spoke. "Larry, just what exactly do you think you're doing? Gordy seems to be running away with the ball and I'm not even sure what game we're playing."

"Who cares?" Larry responded in an intense whisper. "We've got him nibbling. Let's reel him in and worry about whether to fry or bake later."

"Larry," Laura whispered back, "let's try this without any allusions to football or fishing, agreed?"

Larry nodded, smiling indulgently.

"Here's the deal as I see it," Laura continued. "This musical-theme idea of Gordy's won't fly. Our ideas will. We need to steer him back on course."

"Look, we can make it work. Hell, Laura. Do you know how much money we're talking about here? For this kind of account we can do anything. First, though, we have to sell Gordy on our agency, and if your little tune will get him signed up . . ."

"Larry, there is no song. I was humming something I heard in a deli."

"What do you mean there's no song?" Larry looked as if he'd just been notified of an IRS audit. "Gordy'll be back here in a minute. What do you mean there's no tune? Our client, our *very lucrative* client, likes that tune."

"It was something I heard some guy singing."

"What guy?"

"Some guy in a deli. I think he's a musician," Laura said evasively.

"A musician who works in a deli?"

"No, I think he's a musician of some sort. I ran into him at Greene's."

"So, run into him again. Offer him a grand for the rights. You know musicians—they're always short of cash. Hell, offer him a job if he wants. If it gets us Universal Foods, I'll make him a vice president. That's better than working in some deli."

"Larry, he doesn't work in the deli. I told you that," Laura answered petulantly. She only became petulant when she knew she was beaten. "He thinks advertising people are the scum of the earth."

Larry looked over his shoulder and saw Gordy wending his way back toward them. "So we're scum of the earth. Write him a check—he'll get over it."

"I don't think so." Laura sighed.

"He's a man, right? Turn on the charm. You deliver the deli man, and I'll deliver Cowboy Bob, there."

LAURA ENTERED Alex's apartment building armed with a sackful of freshly baked bagels and the courage of her convictions. *Money talks. Larry was right about that—* even Alex Shaw had to have his price. After all, he was a young man, and this building wasn't exactly Trump Tower. She'd have to test the waters to see just how little she could get away with.

Laura had left Larry and Mr. Gordy lingering over their *crème brûlées*. None of her subtle attempts to steer Gordy toward more palatable strategies had worked, so she'd given up and headed straight for Shaw's apartment. She knew full well that in these early stages of seducing a potential client, even the slightest crossed signal could be fatal. If Gordy wanted the damned tune, she'd get him the damned tune. Later, she'd convince him of the error of his ways.

In the center of the lobby an older man sat behind a tall semicircular desk. A long, tangled white wire stretched like an umbilical cord from his left ear to a tiny portable TV.

Laura peered over the desk. He was watching pro wrestling.

"Can you buzz Mr. Alex Shaw's apartment for me, please?"

"And you are?" the man inquired, eyes glued to the TV.

"I am—" She hesitated. It had been several days. Would he even remember her name? "Tell him it's the woman who gave the world Yum-Yums."

"So *you're* the bum." He peered at her over the rims of thick black-framed glasses. "You ever tasted those things?"

"Well, yes—"

"Like chewing on a piece of chalk. Disgusting. Couldn't you make it more like, say, Juicy Fruit?"

Laura smiled in spite of herself. "We're still working out the kinks. I'll pass along your suggestion. And Mr. Shaw?" She nodded toward the intercom console.

He pushed a buzzer, then waited. No answer. "You know, he's probably up in the gym. Usually is, this time of day. That guy works out like some people go to church. Never misses a day."

"Well, can I go up there? It's really very important."

"Yeah, what the hey. You look pretty harmless."

"Many men have regretted thinking that." Laura laughed. "Here, have a bagel." She reached into the bag.

"Thanks. Floor nineteen, turn right out of the elevator."

"I'll just follow my nose."

As she rode up in the elevator, Laura examined her reflection in the brass doors. She looked uncharacteristically tense, and there were telltale frown lines around her mouth. Her stomach was being most uncooperative, lurching in a queasy motion that had nothing to do with the elevator. She tried to convince herself that it was a result of lunch.

But, no. The truth was, she wasn't looking forward to seeing Mr. Shaw again. Not at all. She'd been like him once—brash, opinionated. Well, okay, she still was; but she knew her tongue was a lethal weapon and she chose her targets with care. This guy thought he had a handle on the whole world. He'd heard one word—*advertising*—and figured he had her pegged.

She hated being labeled that way. She was a lot more complex than ten minutes of chitchat in a deli could possibly convey. He'd had a way of looking at her as if he wanted to get the classification down right before pinning her in her place, permanently. At his age everything seemed so much simpler. And anyway, what did Alex Shaw know about advertising?

The elevator hit the nineteenth floor. Laura followed the signs leading to the exercise room, marching along at her standard brisk pace. This whole thing was ridiculous, but if she had to do it, at least she'd do it efficiently. She'd negotiated with corporate barons. Surely she could negotiate with a youngster for the rights to his two-bit jingle. She could handle anybody—

Anybody, perhaps, but not that *body,* she thought after she opened the door to the gymnasium.

Alex Shaw was wearing a pair of maroon gym shorts and some running shoes. But it was not what he *was* wearing that made her forget how to stand.

The room was larger than she'd expected and was filled with complicated pieces of equipment that reminded her of a jungle gym for adults. A large woman in a pink leotard rode an exercise bike while reading a paperback. Two middle-aged men on treadmills were sweating profusely.

Alex was working on a machine that required him to lift a huge—to Laura, impossibly huge—stack of weights by pulling down on a metal bar. He sat on a small bench, his back to her, straining with each pull, as the weights rose in the air.

It was a grueling way to spend an afternoon, but the exercise had very definitely paid off. Except for an eight-inch scar running parallel to his spine, Alex was perfect—a textbook example of male anatomy.

The stirrings of desire she felt were undeniable, but she ignored them and reminded herself exactly why she was here. Still she made no move. Just watching Alex was making breathing difficult—all those muscles, moving with such calculated precision and grace. What was that muscle by the shoulder blade? The something-zoid, wasn't it?

"Are you looking for someone?" the woman on the bicycle asked.

"Y-yes," Laura stammered. "Well—him." She pointed toward Alex. He twisted around, did a double take, then slowly released his hold on the weight machine.

He stood and turned toward her, wiping his hands on his gym shorts.

Oh, Lord. The flip side was even better.

He held out his hand. "Ms....Daniels, wasn't it?" he asked with an easy grin. "Selling door-to-door, are we?"

"Here." She thrust the bag of bagels into his outstretched hand. "I come in peace." She returned his smile, dropping her eyes just long enough to take in his smooth, sculpted chest with its sprinkling of hair curling enticingly at the breastbone.

"Onion. My favorite." He sniffed at the bag. "But—" he peered at her with such intense curiosity that her skin prickled "—why a peace offering? I didn't realize we were at war. Who fired the first shot?"

"Gee." Laura tapped her finger on her chin. "Is it just my imagination or do I recall something about selling my soul?"

Alex bit into one of the bagels. "Maybe I was a little hard on you. Still, there's the matter of the Yum-Yums to be considered. The case against you is strong."

This time it was Alex's turn to drop his gaze, but his survey of Laura's body was far more leisurely. When he made it back to her eyes, what Laura saw in his made her reach for the support of an exercise-bike handlebar. She held on for dear life.

What she'd seen in his eyes was desire.

That was just what she was feeling herself.

"Of course," Alex continued in a bantering tone, "you weren't exactly kind to my impromptu performance. 'Off, off, Broadway,' I believe you said."

"Three *off*s, if I remember correctly."

"Which would put me where? In Newark?"

Laura laughed. "Believe it or not, your little tune's the reason I stopped by."

"There aren't any more verses." He took a step closer. His brow was damp, his face flushed from his exertion.

What a coincidence! She was feeling pretty flushed herself. Not to mention damp, in all kinds of unexpected places.

"Is that really the reason you're here?" he asked softly.

She kept her grip on the bicycle and cleared her throat. "Yes, as strange as it may sound."

He flashed her a wicked grin.

"Is there a place we can talk privately?" Laura suggested.

"Downstairs. My place." He reached for a towel and draped it around his neck. "Shouldn't we be 'doing lunch,' though? I thought all the megadeals were made at the Quilted Giraffe. Or is it the Four Seasons this week?"

"Please, spare me the sarcasm." She followed him into the hallway. "And who said anything about a deal?"

"Just an instinct," he said, leading the way to the elevator.

"Well, save your instincts for the lottery. I just want to talk."

Alex pressed the Down button and within seconds the elevator arrived. They stepped inside, each retreating to a corner.

"You people live to make deals," Alex goaded her.

"What do you mean, 'you people'? How can you categorize me when you barely know my name?"

"Oh, I see you," Alex stated. "You and all the other little worker bees of Manhattan, buzzing around trying to see who can build the biggest hive."

Before Laura could retort, the elevator doors opened and they stepped into a semidark hallway, lit by a few brass wall sconces.

Alex's apartment was the first on their right. He stooped down and retrieved a key from his running shoes. "I'm a little short of pockets," he explained.

"I noticed," Laura replied, immediately regretting the flirtatious tone of her voice.

The apartment was small by Laura's standards, but pleasant. The living room was dominated by a large picture window, just as Laura knew all too well it would be. And in the center of the room was the baby grand piano she'd watched him play. Staff paper covered with handwritten music was spread out over its gleaming ebony top.

To her right was a tidy eat-in kitchen, and to her left, a half-open door revealing an unmade bed. The piano was definitely the focus of the apartment. On the wall nearest to her was a ceiling-high storage unit filled to capacity with albums, compact discs and books. Two expensive-looking stereo speakers were suspended on the walls, and an elaborate sound system dominated one corner.

"Have a seat," Alex offered. "Assuming that you can find one. I'm afraid I don't do a lot of entertaining."

"Well, this is business."

"I know." Alex shook his head and headed toward the bathroom. "Believe me, you've made that abundantly clear." He turned back toward her. "Listen, there're sodas in the fridge. I have to jump into the shower for a minute. Keep talking. I'll leave the door open so I can hear you."

He disappeared from sight, leaving Laura standing uncomfortably in the main room. A moment later she heard the shower running and the sound of a sliding-glass door closing.

"So, what's the pitch?" Alex called.

"No pitch—" Laura began.

"Can't hear you. What?"

Laura stepped closer to the tantalizingly open door. She caught a glimpse of the frosted-glass of the shower door before stopping. "No pitch," she repeated loudly. "A simple business proposition. A client of mine may be interested in that little 'bagel' ditty of yours."

"You're kidding." Alex laughed. "What, was he in the deli the other day?"

"No."

"Then how the hell could he want to buy a tune he's never heard? Who told him about it, anyway?" Alex seemed amused.

"I did," Laura answered lightly, wandering back to the living room, where she casually examined a wall shelf loaded with books. If she turned her head to the right—

"Liked it that much, did you?"

"No. Actually, I was just humming it and he overhead it. The client thought it was . . . pleasant."

"Pleasant enough for you to show up on my doorstep unannounced."

She couldn't see his face, but she could make a guess at the smirk that accompanied that statement. She turned away from her perusal of his books, not really looking toward the bathroom door, but not exactly looking away. She felt a wave of disappointment when she saw nothing but a cloud of steam.

"Believe me," she continued, "I would have called, but you're not listed."

The sound of running water stopped and again she heard the door sliding open. The image that came to mind made her squirm. She took a deep breath that did nothing to steady her.

The bathroom door opened, letting a vaporous cloud escape. In the middle of the cloud Alex appeared, wearing a short blue terry cloth robe.

"That's right," he said, suddenly suspicious. "I'm not listed. So, how did you know where I live?"

How did she know where he lived? Because she had seen him standing at his window; had watched him from afar and let her imagination run wild thinking of that broad back, those strong arms. But she couldn't exactly admit *that*, could she? After all, it was his business if he wanted to parade around shirtless in view of a half-million New Yorkers. But there was no way she could ever admit—

Think fast, Laura.

"Mrs. Greene down at the deli. She told me you lived upstairs." Would he buy that?

"Oh." He nodded noncommittally.

Close, Laura. She was losing control of this negotiation. Time to reassert herself. She made a show of looking at her watch. "I'm going to be late. And as much as I'm not enthusiastic about getting back to work, I do have to set a good example. So, let me put this to you as a simple business proposition."

"I'm listening," he replied solemnly.

"We often use free-lancers for jingles. This particular client has some ideas that probably won't fly. With any luck at all he'll come to his senses, but in the interim he wants your tune to be the centerpiece . . . to be part of a campaign we're working on. Interested?"

Alex nodded. "Just for the sake of argument, what kind of money are we talking about, here?"

She had him. "Big. Enough to keep you in staff paper for years."

"Naturally," Alex mused, walking over to the piano and trailing a finger along the keyboard, "I'd look like a hypocrite taking money from a company I've lampooned."

"No," Laura encouraged him. "Just a realist. We all have to eat, right?" She paused. "Do you have a job, by the way?"

Alex winced, obviously ill at ease. "Um, I play piano in a little jazz club in Greenwich Village. And I have some money put away from—" He stopped himself from saying anything more. "I have some savings. Not much."

He went to the window and stood, hands on hips, staring out. It was a pose Laura was familiar with.

"I don't know. I could use the money, but I wouldn't feel right," he continued softly.

From the tone of his voice Laura knew he *was* serious. "It's just a jingle for an ad, Alex," she reminded him. "You won't be peddling land mines to toddlers."

"What would I be selling—if I were selling, that is?"

"Well, it's for Universal Foods. They market a series of products—frozen food, specialty items, floor-care products."

"The *equivalents* of Yum-Yums." Alex shook his head. She liked how his loose waves of hair grazed his neck as he moved. "Look, Laura," he said uncertainly, "I won't lie to you. I could use the money. Really use it. But this isn't what I expected to do when I worked my butt off for

my composition degree. I mean, I knew I wasn't going
into the most lucrative field in the world, but still, I
wanted to write real music—good music."

"Fine," Laura answered abruptly—*Let him think he's
lost it.* "I can see I'm wasting my time here. I'll give you
my card, and if you reconsider you can give me a call. If
not, well, it's been . . . most interesting."

Great Laura! Corrupt his youthful idealism. He took
the card from her hand and looked at it carefully.

"Well!" He whistled. "Corporate vice president. Very
impressive."

"You know," Laura responded to his sarcasm with
more force than she'd intended, "I didn't have to come
here. I knew you'd be too cocky to be dealt with reasonably."

"'Cocky,' eh?" The accusation seemed to please him.
"I thought that was part of the game. Playing hard to get,
and all."

"Well, you're out of your league, mister," Laura
warned.

"Maybe so. I'll bet you wrote the book on playing hard
to get. But wait—you were talking about business,
weren't you?"

His flirtatious tone caught her off guard. Maybe he
wasn't so far out of his league. He certainly was able to
throw her off easily enough. Even now, she couldn't tell
whether she'd hooked him or not.

"Like I said, give me a call." She turned to leave.

"Who exactly would I be working with?" he asked
softly.

*Got him. So why didn't she feel triumphant? Why did
she feel so unnerved?*

"Why, me, primarily. That is, if you want to participate in adapting your music. Just for a short time, you understand."

"Time is relative," he answered cryptically. "Tell you what—I'll sleep on it, okay?"

"Good." Laura nodded. Game, set and match. He'd come around. She'd achieved her main objective and Larry would be happy. Of course, Larry wouldn't be the one having to work closely with Alex; she would. At least in the office he'd be wearing a shirt. That should make it somewhat easier. She would have to make it very, very clear that their relationship was strictly business. She didn't want to be known around the office as a cradle robber. It was bad enough that people knew she was consulting a matchmaker, let alone eyeing some man young enough to be—

How old was he, anyway? Could he be as old as his late twenties?

She blurted out, "How old *are* you, anyway?"

"Twenty-two," Alex said matter-of-factly. "How old are you?"

"Too old."

She put her hand on the door handle. Suddenly she felt the touch of his hand on her cheek. Slowly she turned toward him, overpoweringly aware of his body, his eyes, his fingers tracing the line of her cheek.

Oh, my God. He's going to kiss me.

More shocking still was the realization that she was going to let him.

Alex came closer; Laura's eyes began to close and her lips parted. Nothing happened. She looked into his eyes and was amazed at what she saw there. He was afraid.

"Umm," he stammered, looking down and letting his hand drop away. "I'll, uh—I'll call you."

Laura headed away down the hall, mystified and annoyed.

Silly, she chided herself. Good grief! He was twenty-two. And she was thirty-five. Thirty-five minus twenty-two was thirteen.

And thirteen—as anyone could tell you—was a very unlucky number.

3

DESPITE THE FACT that she'd spent most of the night thinking about Alex Shaw, Laura resolved that she would not think about him anymore. Period. End of story. It wasn't even a kiss, after all. Just what? A pass? If it was a pass, it was definitely an incomplete one.

Of course she was asking the impossible of herself. It was like trying not to think about chocolate while you were on a diet.

It came as no real surprise that she continued to think about Alex as she showered the next morning. She thought about him while brushing her teeth. She softly sang, "'You must remember this, a kiss is just a kiss . . .'" during the cab ride to work.

She thought about Alex during the morning staff meeting at work. She thought about him during a call to a Tokyo client. She thought about him at the most inappropriate moments.

When she glanced up from a pile of spreadsheets to see his lean figure in the doorway, she thought—for a split second—that it was just a trick of her mind.

"Very chichi," he said in a low voice.

So it was him!

"Bet you had to sell a hell of a lot of Yum-Yums to get here."

He was clad in a pair of form-fitting jeans, faded to flannel softness at the knees, along with a black T-shirt, running shoes and a tweed jacket—a casual look that

Laura found appealing. Even his hair was tousled. He was definitely in need of a shave.

"You look like you just dragged yourself out of bed," Laura commented, almost managing to sound indifferent.

"Haven't been to bed, actually. Musicians keep odd hours."

"So," Laura asked, "did you sleep on my offer?"

Before he could respond, Larry appeared behind Alex in the doorway. He wrapped his arm around Alex like he was his long-lost son. "Laura, this guy's dynamite," Larry enthused. "How'd you find him?"

"Umm—" Laura cleared her throat "—I keep my eyes open."

"Well, he's on board now. He's going to work up some possibilities along the lines Gordy was discussing. Then I thought we could have a conference at my place this weekend."

"We ... who?"

"Oh, you know. The usual suspects. Your whole group, Silverman—to go over some preliminary ideas on the media buys, and Rhoda, if she's up to it. And our boy Alex, here."

"Of course." Her eyes darted over to Alex's face. His Tom Sawyer grin was for her benefit.

"Alex—" Larry gave him a one-of-the-guys handshake. "Glad to have you with us. You have any questions, Laura here will show you the ropes."

"Ropes, eh?" Alex raised one eyebrow. "I doubt they'll be necessary."

Larry's eyes clouded, as they always did when a conversation veered even momentarily off track. "Yes. Well ... gotta run."

Once Larry was gone Laura let her head sink down onto the desk. Larry's "conferences" were a notorious staple of corporate life at Tate and O'Neill. They sounded fine in theory: a weekend at his Long Island estate, with work thrown in between clambakes and volleyball games. Unfortunately, they tended to end in a debacle of one sort or another. Laura felt that business should be conducted in the office, but she went along, as the others did. But bring Alex along? He would just confuse things.

Alex stepped into her office. He examined a Jim Dine print on her wall, then sauntered over to take a look inside the ebony bar unit.

"Do come in," Laura intoned.

"Don't mind if I do," he responded, thumbing through the current copy of *AdWeek* on her coffee table.

"Don't waste much time, do you?"

"What's that?"

"Last I heard, you were decidedly undecided about our offer."

"Well, I slept on it, like you said. Had a helluva good dream, too. You were working out on the Nautilus and—"

"Spare me the details, okay?"

"Okay." Alex shrugged. "Let's just say you were in really great shape."

She ignored him and toyed with a paper clip.

Alex moved to the center of the room, thumbs hooked in his belt loops. "I don't know." He shook his head. "This isn't you."

She liked the stark black-and-white color scheme, the sleek lines of the contemporary leather couch and chairs. She often wished the rest of her world could be this serene and uncomplicated. "Funny," she mused, "I was laboring under the impression that this *was* my office."

"Naw." Alex dragged a chrome chair over to her desk and dropped onto it. "This is some tony decorator's version of you. You're more primary colors."

"Kindergarten-classroom style?"

He laughed, tossing his head back. "Tell you what, though. I like the view." He stood again and marched over to the wall of glass behind her.

"It's like your view," she pointed out.

"Only your window's the size of a football field." He peered across the street.

Laura couldn't help but notice that one of his tattered jeans pockets was hanging on for dear life. That wasn't all she registered about that general vicinity, but it was the only data she would acknowledge.

"I'll be damned! My apartment is directly across from here," Alex commented.

Laura glanced over her shoulder quickly. "So it is," she said nonchalantly, but her voice betrayed her by rising like a junior high school girl's.

Alex seemed about to say something more, but evidently decided to let it pass.

"So, you and Larry are *real* pals," Laura observed, changing the subject.

"I had a football coach like him in high school. Real gung-ho. A true believer."

"Football? What position did you play?"

"Fullback," he answered softly, his face clouding.

He stepped closer and sat on the corner of her desk. It was a move that ordinarily would have enraged her—she guarded her territory—but this time she welcomed the invasion.

Laura decided to make yet another effort to push the conversation back toward business. "Did you and Larry discuss any specifics? About how long you'll be with the Universal Foods project?"

"He gave me the old 'this could be the start of something big' speech. Short on specifics, but he probably figures I'm some kid from the sticks who'll work for the thrill of it. That's okay. We'll get along fine. The thing about Larry is, he's so transparent that you can't help but like him."

Five minutes with Larry and Alex had him pegged. If nothing else, he was a good judge of character. And not one to mince words. She had to admire that.

"Isn't this your cue to tell me what a hypocrite I am?" Alex asked.

Laura stifled a smile. "The word *sellout* did come to mind."

"That all depends on what the payoff is. Every man has his price."

"Well, I told you that advertising can be very lucrative."

"I'm sure it can be." Alex got off Laura's desk, staring down at her with a mixture of frustration and amusement. "I wasn't talking about money."

She looked up at him, forcing herself not to encourage his flirtation.

"Well, gotta go," he announced suddenly. "Larry says you guys have a computer-augmented synthesizer in a studio right here in the building. That's a little more high-tech than I'm used to, but it'll be fun to figure it out."

"Do you even have any idea where to start?" Laura asked.

"With the synthesizer?"

"No, I meant with the project itself."

"Sure." He nodded. "I figure it's like doing music for a TV series or a movie. You start with a theme and then build on it. For example, take the opening music for *Dallas*. The theme is played at different tempos according to need—for romance, action, or suspense. But basically it's the same thematic melody."

"Yes," Laura agreed. "That's what Gordy wants, but it won't be easy. Each product has to be represented by a strong piece of music. So you're talking about a dozen or more jingles with a common theme that the average person will hear and say, 'Oh, yeah! They must be part of Universal Foods.'"

"Yeah." Alex grinned happily. "It's a real bitch. In fact, it's an almost-impossible job—that's a big part of the reason I decided to do it. The impossible music and—" he favored her with a lascivious look "—the impossible dream."

Laura watched as he walked out and disappeared from view. In the hallway she could see a pair of secretaries turn 180 degrees to watch him walk away.

"A trifle cocky, aren't we, Mr. Shaw?" Laura muttered. She wasn't sure she liked the idea of working with him. No, she *knew* she didn't like the idea. On the subject of men, she was fallible. But when it came to work, her instincts were deadly accurate. And this arrangement was not going to fly. Alex was too...disruptive for her to tolerate for long. But this project could easily go on for months. And beyond this project, Larry could go on using him as he did the agency's other free-lancers.

She was probably worrying for nothing. Alex would never last in this environment.

So, why had he signed on at all? Why had he taken up her offer? For the challenge? Maybe. More likely for the money.

"I wasn't talking about money," he said.

Out of sheer perversity, then.

If there was some other reason, she didn't want to acknowledge it.

"Here's the Universal file you wanted." Rhoda appeared in the doorway, wearing a frilly pink maternity dress bedecked with bows. She handed a thick folder to Laura, then brushed at her lace collar with irritation.

"New dress?" Laura asked.

"Don't start on me." Rhoda smiled ironically. "A gift from my mom. Figured I'd wear it once, then pretend it shrank in the wash."

"My lips are sealed."

"Why do they always make maternity dresses that look like something a Chatty Cathy would wear?"

"Chatty Cathy? Rhoda, you're dating yourself."

"Hey, I've got a few good years left before they put me out to pasture." She turned to leave, then appeared to change her mind. "Speaking of years . . . I wonder how old Alex is?"

"Twenty-two."

"You asked?"

"Just in passing."

"Well, that's no big deal." Rhoda shrugged. "Thirteen years."

Laura chewed on her pen. "Just what are you suggesting, Rhoda?"

"Nothing. I was just pointing out that you and he are really pretty close to the same age."

"In dog years, maybe." Laura laughed. "Listen, did you take care of everything for this evening?"

"You mean for the great evaluation by Margo Morgenroth? The meeting where she decides who you are, what you are, and whether you're going on her 'A' list, to be hooked up with the greatest studs of New York City, or on her 'Z' list, condemning you to an endless stream of dates with losers you'd rather die than go out with?"

"That would be funny if it weren't very nearly the truth. What if she thinks I'm too overbearing or bitchy? What if she hooks me up with some potbellied old man? What will that say about me?"

"Boy, you are worked up about this," Rhoda observed. "Why can't you just meet this woman in her office?"

"I wish I could, but the mighty Ms. Morgenroth likes to see her potential clients in their home environment. Gives her a better feel for their true personality."

"Well, don't worry. The cleaning service has been there all day, so she'll never know the awful truth," Rhoda joked. "And I took care of everything on your list: flowers by Renny, specifically, alstroemeria and irises; hors d'oeuvres from the Silver Palate—to wit, a nice country pâté and Camembert; and I had a framed picture of me delivered and placed on your side table."

"A picture of you? Why?"

"To make it look like you have at least one personal friend. Wouldn't do for you to look like you're all business."

"Good thinking." Laura smiled. "By the way, if you were looking for a picture of a friend, you chose the right picture."

FOR A CHANGE Laura actually left the office at five o'clock. She wanted to be sure everything was in order for the matchmaker and allow herself plenty of time for a long, hot shower.

Her co-op looked stunning, like something out of *Architectural Digest*. The living room seemed more welcoming than usual, probably because of the huge Waterford vase brimming with the fresh flowers. She'd had the room done over last year when her promotion became official. It was designed for entertaining by a highly recommended decorator; the focal point was a "conversation pit" of Italian couches done in a striped chintz in off-white and—what had the decorator insisted on calling that color?—"apricot brandy." Laura really didn't have the time to devote to poring over fabric swatches and carpet samples. And yet the room sometimes reminded her of a Creamsicle. When the decorator had asked about her bedroom, she'd laid down the law.

Her bedroom was her sanctuary—her private, peaceful haven. The room was a decorator's nightmare—a riot of uncoordinated colors: a royal blue satin quilt and red and yellow throw pillows messily covered the king-size bed. The walls were layered with memorabilia. There was the tie-dyed T-shirt from her first Grateful Dead concert; the ebony tribal mask from Africa; the Girl Scout award she won in fifth grade for the most cookie sales—even then she'd had a knack for sales. A small basketball hoop was attached to her closet door. She'd been a center in high school.

The room represented the part of her that had never fully accepted that she was a mature adult woman. The bedroom was defiantly hers alone. Besides, it wasn't as if she did a whole lot of entertaining in there.

Laura stripped off her clothes, threw them carelessly onto the bed, and headed in her slip to the kitchen. There she chose a frozen entrée from the selection she had delivered each week by her favorite wine-and-cheese shop. The instructions advised eight minutes in the microwave.

Good. Plenty of time for a shower. She popped the entrée into her microwave and set the timer for eight minutes.

The shower was sheer, luxurious relief. Nothing seemed worth worrying about. Maybe she and the matchmaker would hit it off. Maybe Margo Morgenroth knew some gorgeous, brilliant CEO of a Fortune 500 company who adored anchovy pizzas and mature, successful women. Then again, maybe Margo was a rip-off artist who saw a market and had decided to exploit it.

Laura poured a dollop of almond-scented shampoo into her palm and massaged it into her scalp. There was no point in copping an attitude this early in the game. She would have to keep an open mind. Rhoda claimed everyone had a perfect soul mate on earth and it was just a matter of tracking him or her down. Maybe Margo had some inside information.

Laura had never been an early-to-rise type, and years of racing against the clock to make it to work on time had made her a quick-change artist. She was ready within a half an hour, a full hour before Margo was due to arrive. Plenty of time to eat a relatively leisurely dinner and hide the dishes away in the dishwasher.

Her food was done and only needed a thirty-second warm-up. She was just punching the buttons when she heard her intercom buzzer. A wisp of panic blew over her. Was Margo there already?

No, Margo wasn't the type to show up an hour early. That would be too impolite.

"Damn it." She marched over to the door-side intercom. "Yeah?" she barked.

The voice was tinny and indistinct, but the tune was familiar:

"I got Glo-wax—
It's a no-wax.
I got Glo-wax—
Who could ask for anything more?"

Alex was singing jingles in her lobby?

"Alex?" she asked, not quite trusting her ears.

"So, whaddya think?"

"I think even Fred Astaire would've flopped with those lyrics."

"They suck?"

Laura laughed. "That's being charitable. May I ask what you're doing here?"

"I thought we could run some ideas up the flagpole and see how they fly. Get all our ducks in a row—"

"Say what?"

"Sorry. I thought that's how you types talked."

"You need to get out of the house more often. Look, I'm a little busy here. See me at the office tomorrow."

"No, really. I've got a couple of great ideas, and tomorrow's Friday. I wanted to get your feedback before I flesh them out for this weekend at Larry's."

Mother told me there'd be days like this. She never said anything about weeks.

"Alex. I've got a seven-thirty appointment."

"Five minutes. Tops."

At this rate, she'd spend at least that long just trying to get rid of him.

"Fine. That's it, though."

She pressed the button to let him into the lobby below, and turned to check herself in the mirror. Well, at least she was dressed to receive company. Five minutes earlier and he would have caught her without makeup—

and she certainly wasn't ready for that. Although that would have put an end to his flirtation.

She heard a knock at the door and remembered the dinner in her microwave. She was starving. Maybe she could get rid of him quickly and still have time—

He knocked again, more insistently. Laura hesitated at the door, then checked her peephole. It was Alex, all right, in fish-eye distortion—all head, with tiny limbs. She unlocked her dead bolt and released the safety chain.

"How did you find me, anyway?" she asked by way of hello, blocking his entrance. "I'm not in the book."

"Wild guess." He smiled engagingly. "Isn't this the part where you invite me in?"

Laura flung open the door. "Oh, what the hell. Let's get this over with."

"That's the spirit." Alex entered with a swagger. He was wearing the same faded jeans from that morning— she recognized the loose pocket—and a dark green flannel shirt the color of his eyes. And he still hadn't shaved apparently, which gave him a rebel-without-a-cause scruffiness she found devastating and . . . dangerous.

Alex surveyed the room with the same derisive sneer he'd exhibited in her office. "Same decorator, right?"

"Look—" Laura bridled "—when I want your opinion on interior decorating, I'll ask for it."

"Reminds me of a Creamsicle." He moved to sit on one of the couches, then hesitated. "May I? Or are these just props?"

Laura waved him off. She felt a strong craving for the Chardonnay in her refrigerator. "Wine?" she asked Alex over her shoulder.

"Great."

She returned with two cut-crystal wineglasses and handed one to Alex.

"Thanks," he said, then gave a low whistle, nodding at the platter of crackers already artistically arrayed on the coffee table awaiting Margo's arrival. "You shouldn't have gone to such trouble, really," Alex remarked, almost convincing her he was serious.

"I told you, I have a seven-thirty appointment." She sat down on the couch across from him. It *was* rather uncomfortable.

"Client?"

"No, not that it's any of your business."

"I *am* practically a member of the firm," Alex reminded her with mock pride. "So, male or female?"

"Alex!"

"Must be male, the way you're dressed."

Laura took a sip of her wine and disregarded his comment. "Subtle hints don't work well with you, do they?" she observed.

"Naw. Sledgehammer's generally a better tactic."

"Don't tempt me."

"Don't tell me anyone's ever accused *you* of being subtle, Ms. Daniels. You're about as subtle as a steamroller."

"Thanks."

"No, no—I like that in a woman." Alex lifted the corner of a piece of plastic wrap protecting a ring of crackers. "You mind if I scarf one of these? I haven't eaten since the hot dog I had at Nathan's this morning for breakfast. Best dogs in the free world, by the way."

Laura laughed. "With chili, yeah. At least we agree on something." She slouched back onto the rigid couch cushions. Against her better judgment, she was relaxing. "Oh, go ahead."

Alex pulled off the wrap and removed a couple of crackers, then handed the plate to Laura.

"I can rearrange it later," she muttered, grabbing herself a handful. "So, what was the big breakthrough? I really am in kind of a hurry."

"I hear you." Alex nodded. "But I did want to run this by you before I went ahead with it." He swallowed a cracker and stood. "Mind if I use the piano?"

"No," she said. "Go right ahead."

"You play?" he asked with curiosity as she followed him, carrying her wineglass, to the piano in the far corner of the room.

"Not really. It functions primarily as a plant stand." Actually, her decorator had begged her to sell it, but she'd insisted on keeping the old upright, which had belonged to her grandmother. Now she was glad she had.

"You should learn," Alex advised. "Maybe I could give you a few lessons."

"I've had lessons," she explained. "Things were going fine until my first recital. I was all set to deliver this really inspired rendition of 'Twinkle, Twinkle, Little Star.' Took one look at the audience and nearly wet my pants."

Alex clucked his tongue. "It's happened to all the greats. Cliburn, Horowitz, Ax—"

"You?"

"Well, no." He shook his head apologetically. "Of course, I have remarkable self-control. But I will admit that chili dogs were out of the question the day of my first club appearance. Say, all this good talk is making me hungry. Mind if I raid your refrigerator?"

"Uh, well, no. Go ahead," Laura answered hesitantly. How could she say no without sounding...uptight? Old, even? Besides, she was starving herself.

She watched as Alex leaped to his feet and made his way over to the compact kitchen. "Whoa, this looks good," he called out, his head buried in the fridge. "Pâté and Brie. But it looks like company food."

"It's Camembert, actually," Laura corrected him automatically. "And it is for company—" *That's right, Laura*, she chided herself. *Make him feel welcome.* But the spread was for Margo.... "And you're company, and I'm hungry, so bring it on out."

Alex returned with the hors d'oeuvres and two small plates and set them on the piano. "I thought since I was here in Decoratorland I'd use a plate."

"How considerate," Laura said dryly. She prepared a small plate and glanced at the rosewood clock on her sideboard. Six forty-five. Plenty of time to have a little shoptalk with a co-worker and be ready for the Inquisition, as she fatalistically had begun to consider Margo's visit. For some odd reason she was glad of Alex's interruption. Discussing the Universal account would be a pleasant diversion from obsessing over the question of why a perfectly intelligent, attractive woman like herself had been driven to using a matchmaker to find a man.

"Refill?" she asked as Alex sat on the piano bench and tested a few random keys.

"Sure," he murmured, launching into a string of bluesy arpeggios that left her speechless.

She picked up the wine bottle and carried it over to him. He stopped abruptly.

"Oh, don't stop," she pleaded.

"Just warming up." He accepted the glass of wine. "Thanks," he said, sliding over on the piano bench. "Here. Have a seat."

Laura hesitated, then settled in next to him, clutching her glass. Their thighs grazed, and she registered a bewitching tremor running the length of her spine, as smooth and magical as Alex's fingers skating up the keyboard.

"So, anyway," she began throatily, "the Universal account?"

"Lord," Alex commented, "you have the most incredible voice. I suppose you hear that all the time."

Laura shook her head. She *had* heard it before, but not in a very long time. Again, Alex had derailed her.

"It reminds me of—" Alex rubbed his chin, and she suddenly wanted to feel the bristly plane of his jaw for herself "—of Lauren Bacall or Kathleen Turner. Sultry."

"Thanks." Laura felt herself blush and was relieved when Alex returned his attention to the piano. "I think."

"You know, you don't take compliments all that well," he noted.

"Who can tell with you? You just called me a steam-roller."

"Another case in point."

"That's your idea of flattery?" Laura laughed hoarsely.

"It means I find you direct, uncompromising. Sure of yourself. In my book, that's a compliment."

"Hmm," Laura mused. "My boyfriend—ex, that is—called me abrasive. He said assertive women made him nervous."

"How'd you end up together, then?" Alex leaned his elbow on the keys and a couple of dissonant *plink*s broke the silence.

"Well, this was several years ago. I was younger than, more malleable. I guess it took a while for Gerald to recognize the real me." Laura nibbled at a cracker. "Or for *me* to recognize the real me. Anyhow..." She trailed off. "We need to wrap this up."

"Okay." Alex smiled patiently and shifted gears. "Here's the deal. We drop the cutesy jingle approach and go for a theme song that's, I dunno, *big*. Something sweeping, orchestral. With class, in other words. Something that makes people stop blabbing over their TV trays and take notice."

"Alex," Laura explained gently, "that's the goal of every TV commercial ever produced."

"Yeah, but they blow it by thinking 'Plop-plop, fizz-fizz' when they should be thinking—"

"What? Wagner?" Laura interrupted. "Oh, Alex, you've got a lot to learn."

"So teach me," he answered huskily, and it was clear that he wasn't talking about advertising.

She had to move. It was imperative that she do something—anything—to break the spell.

She placed her right hand on top of Alex's left, and settled it gently onto the keys. "So," she told him, sounding more sultry than any Lauren Bacall movie *she*'d ever seen, "show me what you mean."

When he began playing, the melody she heard was all the things he'd promised—poignant, sweeping, strikingly memorable.

"Alex," she murmured as the last bars reverberated, "that was exquisite. It was—" at a loss for words, she shook her head "—absolutely beautiful. Perfect."

"Thank you." He nodded, adding teasingly, "Now *that's* how to respond to a compliment."

"But—"

"Whoops. Apparently I responded too soon."

"But that's no more TV material than, say, a minuet. It's completely wrong. I mean, I loved it. But it's all wrong."

"I thought you'd say that." Alex chuckled. "But you'll come around. Give it twenty-four hours."

"I've been in this business a long time, Alex," Laura informed him sharply. "I've got damn good instincts. Gordy'll never go for this. He liked your bagel jingle. That's what he wants. This song would make a great national anthem, maybe. But we're selling floor wax and pickles, not flags."

She hoped she wasn't being too hard on him.

"Sleep on it," he told her, smiling. "That's all I ask. Besides, this melody is based on the bagel song."

Laura pursed her lips. "Larry explained that I *am* the boss, right?"

"He didn't have to."

Laura craned her neck to check the time on Alex's watch. "Oh, Lord," she muttered. "I haven't got much time. Alex, you've got to go."

"Who exactly is this mystery guest who strikes fear in the heart of Laura Daniels?"

"A business associate. And she'll be here any minute—"

"Wait a minute, wait a minute. Time-out. You're having this anxiety attack over a *woman?*" he questioned incredulously.

"It's hardly an anxiety attack," Laura retorted. "Margo Morgenroth is a valued business associate, and as such, I feel—"

"No!" Alex shook his head in disbelief. "No. Tell me there's another one."

"You *know* her?" Laura asked warily. If so, Margo traveled in some quirky social circles.

"I know *of* her. The *Times* did a story on her a while back. 'The matchmaker of choice for Yuppie weasels'?" He scrutinized her face. "No," he pronounced. "Not *you*. A woman like you?" Alex shook his head adamantly. "No way."

"A woman like me?" Laura repeated, her tone expressing curiosity and ire.

"Yeah," Alex said emphatically. "Beautiful. Intelligent." He stopped short then. "You get the idea."

"Alex, my dear." Laura patted him on the shoulder, sighing heavily. "Let me give you a little demographics lesson. You take your basic thirty-five-year-old woman, drop her in the Big City, and the odds are ninety-nine to one that every man she meets will either be married and lying about it, gay and admitting to it, or a psychiatric outpatient."

Alex stared at her as if she were a candidate for the last category. "But a *matchmaker?*"

"Alex, I'm a very busy woman," Laura responded edgily. "I work twelve- to fourteen-hour days. How am I supposed to meet men?"

"Hang out at an army post?" Alex offered with a sarcastic grin. "I don't know, Laura. I hear there are a lot of eligible guys killing time over at Greene's deli."

Why was she sharing this with someone so unsympathetic? She knew Alex couldn't possibly empathize, but she kept on explaining herself.

"You've heard of the ol' biological time clock? Well, mine is ticking so loud I can't sleep nights." She cleared her throat self-consciously. "I can't expect you to understand what I'm talking about."

"I know something about lost time," Alex answered quietly. "It's a scary feeling, thinking you may be missing out on life and there's nothing you can do about it."

Laura wondered what on earth could have made him sound so sad, but she decided against pursuing it. She wanted to lighten the mood, not be drawn into more confidences. "Exactly. That's why I'm taking the bull by the horns, so to speak. I'm not going to find true love, or even just a garden-variety husband, if I don't *look*, right? And if it takes Margo Morgenroth to deliver the goods, so be it."

"How can a complete stranger possibly know who's right for you?" He was leaning toward her with a look of intense curiosity, like an anthropologist studying the customs of a primitive tribesman.

"That's why she's coming here this evening—to get to know me. My likes and dislikes."

"You're kidding, right?"

"No. I'm not." She looked him straight in the eye, determined to convince him she wasn't nuts. "Look, it makes more sense to take control of the situation logically, to strategize, than it does to spend the rest of my life waiting to meet Mr. Perfect in the supermarket produce department."

"That's not real life, Laura," Alex told her calmly. "'Life is what happens to you while you're making other plans.' Ever heard that one? What about fate?"

"I don't have time to wait for fate."

"Such a romantic!" Alex remarked caustically. "I'm not sure you have a choice in these things."

"Well, *I* am."

Alex distractedly plunked out a minor chord. "So, just where does Ms. Morgenroth acquire her pool of applicants?"

"They're handpicked from a select group of referrals." Laura winced, realizing at once how she must have sounded.

"That can lead to serious inbreeding," Alex warned. "The idea is to stir up the gene pool a little, don't you see? And you know what they say about pedigree breeds—"

"I'm waiting with bated breath," Laura prompted.

"They're temperamental," he said. "Untrustworthy. Spoiled."

"Remind me to put those on my 'dislikes' list."

"And on your 'likes' list?" Alex eased a fraction of an inch closer.

"Loyal. Friendly. Able to fetch my slippers." She grimaced. "I don't know, Alex. Intangible qualities."

"Ah." Alex nodded. "That should narrow things down for old Margo."

"I'll know him when I see him."

Alex looked at her and shook his head dubiously.

"I *will*," she repeated, disregarding the doubt in his face.

There was a long pause.

"He should like anchovies," she offered. "And walks in Central Park."

"Uh-huh."

"He should be tall. Physically fit. A nonsmoker."

"Gotcha."

"Comfortable in a corporate environment. Preferably with an advanced degree."

"Any scars, tattoos or other distinguishing marks?"

"Well, you *asked*," she said defensively. "I'm just giving you a rough outline."

"Laura. You're talking about falling in love, not buying a new car."

How could she even be talking this way? Alex wondered. How could she be telling him to his face that there were no men for her? Was she blind, or was he just so unattractive?

No. He was certain that the attraction was mutual. As certain as he could be.

Then was it the age difference that made her keep her distance? Or had she sensed something? Had she guessed? Was the truth apparent to her experienced eye? The thought frightened him.

"I understand that," Laura was saying. "But buying a car isn't an entirely bad analogy. There are certain features, like air conditioning in a car or a sense of humor in a man. A comfortable interior in a car, an easygoing personality in a man."

"A big, powerful engine in a car. A big, powerful—"

"Very funny," Laura interrupted, laughing.

He loved it when she laughed. When she laughed she stopped being the corporate wonder-woman and was transformed into the free spirit he considered the real Laura Daniels.

But laughter could cut both ways. He wanted to take her in his arms and kiss her. Desperately. But what if she laughed at him? What if the image of him as her lover appeared ridiculous to her?

How could he tell what was in her heart? The other day, in his apartment as she was leaving, he'd thought...hoped...imagined that she'd wanted him to kiss her almost as much as he had wanted it.

You chickened out, Alex! And it wasn't just a question of whether she wanted him. He wasn't exactly Mr. Suave and Experienced. The last woman he'd kissed had been a sixteen-year-old girl who'd had to take the gum out of her mouth first. Even then, he'd felt naive and inexperienced. But now?

The buzzer sounded and he jerked his head toward the sound.

"That would be Margo," Laura said.

"Oh. Well, I guess I should get going." He stood reluctantly and moved away from the piano.

It was now or never.

"Listen, it was fun," she told him, smiling. "I don't know if it's you or the wine, but I feel more relaxed for this interview."

She was *beautiful*. He could reach out and touch her—now. But Laura turned away and led him toward the door.

"Ms. Morgenroth?" Laura inquired into the intercom.

"Yes," came the tinny reply.

"I'll buzz you in. Please come on up."

Only seconds remaining. He searched for something to say. "I...uh, I..." His heart was pounding as if it were trying to break out of his chest. She was near him now, holding her glass of wine. The flavor of it would be on her lips.

"Well," he managed thickly, "I guess I'll see you at work."

Her scent made his legs shake. He reached for the door handle and pulled it open with numb fingers. Other parts of him were anything but numb. His jeans were so tight that if she looked down—

You're behaving like a child! Be a man!

He was already in the hallway outside the door. What was that expression on her face? Desire? Disappointment? Impatience? What?

"Yes, I'll see you at work," she replied.

Was her voice as loaded with emotion as his own, or was he imagining? She was about to turn away. About to close the door. If this moment passed, he might never recapture it.

—What if she laughed at him? What if—

"Oh, to hell with it," he said aloud. He stepped toward her, passing his left arm around her waist and drawing her to him. The fingers of his right hand entwined themselves in her soft, fragrant hair. He noticed her eyes fluttering closed.

Her lips. Her mouth. Her tongue. The feel of her breasts flattened against his chest. The shock as he pressed her body so deliberately against his hardness.

He was going to pass out or explode. It had been so long. Seven endless, pain-racked, fearful years since he had touched—

The wineglass had fallen forgotten from Laura's hand onto the soft carpet. He felt her hands pulling him closer, sweeping across his back.

She was definitely not laughing at him.

No more waiting! He would die if he did not lift her up into his arms and take her—

"Ms. Daniels?"

Suddenly she was pushing him away. He registered the presence of another person—a middle-aged woman wearing an oversize hat.

"Oh! Yes, yes," Laura gasped. "I'm Laura Daniels."

"Well, then, Ms. Daniels," Margo Morgenroth asked, "why on earth do you need me?"

4

LAURA PRESSED DOWN on the accelerator and her black Jaguar leaped up the entry ramp onto the Henry Hudson Parkway traveling north from Manhattan.

Beside her in the passenger seat, Alex was uncharacteristically subdued. He glanced nervously at the speedometer and back over his shoulder at the cars all going over the speed limit.

"Relax," Laura said without taking her eyes off the road. "I'm really a very good driver."

"Yeah, I'm sure you are. It's just that there's a lot of traffic."

"This? This isn't traffic. Try doing this during rush hour. We'd all be going about ten miles an hour."

"That sounds good," Alex muttered.

Was he actually nervous about her driving? Why would he be? Maybe he didn't like driving at all. Or maybe...

"You're not telling me you don't trust women drivers, are you?"

"No, no," he responded quickly. "It's...nothing. Forget it." He swallowed hard. "So," he asked, "how far to Larry's place?"

"He's up near New Canaan, Connecticut. Shouldn't take more than an hour."

"An hour. Okay. That's okay."

As she drove, Laura surreptitiously glanced over at Alex. Alex *was* nervous—not of going to Larry's, but of traveling by car. His right hand was pressed against the rosewood dashboard as if he were bracing himself in his seat. His left hand was clenched in a fist and he'd checked his seat belt at least a half-dozen times since getting in.

She'd heard of people who were phobic about cars. Did Alex have a reason for his fear? She was tempted to ask but she hesitated.

"I was in a car accident," Alex remarked, answering her unspoken question.

"Oh?" Laura responded, trying not to seem excessively interested. "A bad accident?"

"Bad." Alex stared out at the cars around them.

"I wrecked my dad's car when I was sixteen," Laura offered. "No one was hurt except a neighbor's mail-box."

Alex looked at her sharply. "You were lucky."

"I guess I was." She couldn't see any way to gracefully pursue the subject, and Alex had closed himself off from her.

What a strange man! Laura thought. *What a strange young man!*

So young in face and body. So young in his optimism and brashness. Yet he transmitted a maturity born of some battering experience.

Neither of them had mentioned what happened outside her apartment door. But of course, neither had forgotten it. Laura knew *she* hadn't.

The memory sent a shimmer of longing through her. She shifted uncomfortably in her bucket seat and glanced at herself in the rearview mirror. She was embarrassed by her flushed cheeks and her amorous expression.

That one kiss had started a surge of longing coursing through her. Alex could have taken her—then and there.

Thank goodness for Margo Morgenroth's arrival.

If the incident in the hallway proved anything, it wasn't that she wanted Alex, but that she needed a man's love. The *right* man's love. Not the explosive, carnal passions of Alex, but the steady, sensible devotion of an equal and peer.

It didn't take a hundred-and-fifty-dollar-an-hour Manhattan shrink to figure out what her attraction to Alex was all about. She recognized the all-too-familiar symptoms as a variant of what she fondly referred to as the Sinclair Syndrome.

Jerome Sinclair had been her English professor in college; a man nineteen years her senior with an endearing habit of quoting Shakespeare, and a perfectly happy marriage. He was suave, sophisticated and *unattainable*. And she'd been smitten, all the way from Chaucer to Faulkner.

Nothing had come of it. Nothing could *ever* have come of it. And that had been the beauty of the one-sided affair—it was doomed from day one.

There was no difference between Jerome and Alex, aside from a couple of decades and a few strategically located muscles. They were both forbidden and consequently intensely desirable.

It probably didn't hurt that having a near teenager lust after you did wonders for a sagging self-image. No wrinkle cream could compete with the restorative effects that came with realizing a guy who looked like Alex had the hots for you.

Which explained why she'd come within a millimeter of tearing the clothing from his body right there in the hallway.

It was a scary thought. Was she really capable of losing control that way? She stole a glance at Alex, and caught him stealing a glance at her.

Laura looked down self-consciously and realized that her skirt had climbed to midthigh. The snap of her black silk garter was visible. If there was a reason she'd chosen to wear stockings in lieu of panty hose, she preferred not to think about it. Still, if she tugged her skirt down now, it would be clear that she was reacting to Alex, that his gaze meant something to her. That she *wanted* him to look at her, desire her—

"Um, isn't ninety a little fast?"

"Ninety!" Good grief, he was right. The speedometer showed ninety miles per hour. *That*'s what Alex had been glancing at. Well, that would teach her to daydream while she drove. "Oh, sorry, I was off in the ozone."

"Well, there's one good thing." Alex laughed.

"What's that?"

"After that, sixty doesn't make me nervous anymore."

"Good." Laura joined his laughter. "We wouldn't want you nervous."

"Well, then, you'd better pull your skirt down, Laura," he said, "'cause that makes me nervous as hell."

Blushing furiously, Laura tugged at her hem. "Now listen, Alex, we didn't get a chance to talk at the office yesterday about . . . about the other night."

"'The other night'?" He smiled faintly. "I'm surprised you remember the other night. I thought you were going to pretend it never happened."

"It never should have happened." Laura sighed. "You are a very attractive young man, I won't deny that. But you should be out looking for girls your own age. Somehow I don't think you'd have much trouble finding women." She took a deep breath, exhaling it slowly. "Believe me, I'm flattered that you find me attractive, but

I am your boss for the time being. And if nothing else, the firm doesn't exactly approve of office romances."

"Office romances!" Alex laughed. "That conjures up visions of hurried kisses over the copier machine, doesn't it? Maybe quick squeezes in the elevator between floors?"

"You laugh." Laura smiled, relaxing a little. "But last year Larry walked in on an account executive and a copywriter, shall we say, overexposed and subjecting a desk to certain unusual stresses."

"Well, Larry's a big boy," Alex remarked.

"So was the account exec." She paused for effect. "*And* the copywriter. Larry hasn't been quite the same since."

"Did they fire the guys?"

"No. We're all terribly sophisticated, don't you know," Laura replied with a snobbish, upper-class accent. "Nothing shocks a New Yorker."

"What about Larry, then?"

"He was born in South Dakota. They're simpler souls there. He's still capable of being shocked by the big city, even though he's been here for twenty years."

Alex propped his knees against the dashboard, obviously more relaxed. "How about you, Laura?" he asked. "Do you ever get tired of New York?"

Laura looked off to the side. "I guess you get tired of anything sooner or later. New York City has it all—the best entertainment, the best food, the best jobs. There are six different Chinese restaurants that will deliver to my co-op. Cantonese, Hunanese, Mandarin, two Szechuan places . . . Where else can you have that?"

"I don't know. Hong Kong?"

"And if I get up on a Saturday morning and feel like taking in some culture, there's what? About a hundred different museums?"

"How many have you actually been to?" Alex asked, making no effort to hide his skepticism.

Laura hesitated. "Well, I dropped my mom off at the Whitney once when she came to town. And I spent an hour in the Museum of Modern Art. But—"

"I know," Alex interrupted. "You'd do more of that type of thing, but you work all the time."

"Well, someday, when things at the office calm down a little—"

"Things will never calm down. That's the nature of New York. It's so competitive you have to work constantly. So you never really get the chance to enjoy the city."

"Sometimes . . ." She let the word trail off.

"Sometimes what?" Alex pursued.

"Oh, nothing. It's just that I do sometimes think about chucking it all and moving to some small town. Hang up a sign and go into business for myself. Do it all solo, from copywriting to running the accounts. You know, do work for local businesses and radio and TV stations. Maybe a little free-lance writing for firms in the city. Strictly projects that interested me. That's how I got started, you know. In the creative end, writing copy."

"Anywhere special in mind for this small town?" Alex asked, smiling.

"Probably right here in Connecticut, but farther away from the city. Beyond the reach of the smog. Close enough to stay in touch with the action, but far enough away to be able to buy a house." She was talking almost to herself now. "White picket fence. A dog in the yard."

"And a husband?"

"Okay, a husband in the yard, too," she joked self-consciously.

"Kids?"

"Probably not, since I'll be past menopause by the time any of this happens." She forced a laugh, then shrugged philosophically. "Maybe I could adopt, but of course, I'll be older by then. Probably too set in my ways."

"Hmm. And senility right around the corner, no doubt?" Alex japed.

"Yeah. I'll be the nutty old lady who putters around her yard humming the Yum-Yums song."

They were off the highway now and into the green Connecticut countryside.

"Just up around the next corner," Laura said. "And here's a helpful hint, by the way. If Ginger, Larry's wife, tries to get you to play cards, beg off."

"Why?"

"Well, we all think she cheats. But she's so bad at it that she loses anyway. Then she and Larry will have a fight, and you'll get caught in the middle."

"I thought we were just here to work," Alex murmured, looking apprehensive.

"The work is easy, Alex. It's the socializing that will kill you in this racket. There's the place ahead."

LARRY PORTER'S HOME was at the end of a long, paved driveway. The house was a modern, terraced affair, checkered with huge picture windows. To the right, Alex could make out the high chain-link fence that bordered the tennis courts. Beyond that, lying right beside the house, a swimming pool sparkled in the sunlight.

"So," he commented dryly, "I guess advertising *does* pay."

"When you reach Larry's level, yes." Laura looked around, appraising. "Give me another five years and I'll be where he is."

"Unless you blow it all by running off to your mythical little town."

Laura smiled in response.

Which dream held more sway over her? Alex wondered. The house with the dog and the white picket fence or the mansion with the maid and the security gate?

Laura had told him to bring an overnight bag, and as they pulled to a stop in the circular driveway he reached into the back seat to retrieve it.

Alex had never been poor, but this environment did make him uncomfortable. Besides Laura's Jaguar, there were two BMWs and a Cadillac sedan parked at the front. There was also a tan Plymouth that looked about ten years old, with a cheerfully defiant bumper sticker that read, I Need More Money, More Power And Less Crap From You.

He laughed out loud. Following his gaze, Laura explained, "That's Rhoda's car. My secretary. You'll like her."

"I've met her and I already like her," Alex answered.

They climbed the four wide steps to the front door. Laura opened it and walked in. They entered a tiled, high-ceilinged entryway that opened in two directions.

"Ah, Laura! You're here." It was Barry Silverman, a thin, stooped man with a ring of curly hair surrounding a spreading bald patch. "I guess this means we have to get down to work."

"Is that how you regard me, Barry?" Laura bantered. "All work and no play?"

"Well, I did till I saw your . . . friend."

Laura rolled her eyes. "Barry, this is Alex Shaw. He's a free-lance musician working on Universal. Alex, this is Barry Silverman. He's a pain in the ass."

Alex stepped forward and shook Barry's hand.

"Welcome to the fun house," Silverman said. "The great minds are gathered in the living room. Can I get either of you a drink?"

"Black coffee," Laura replied.

Alex hesitated. People judged you by what you ordered in a bar or a restaurant. In the deli, he distinctly remembered Laura had put cream in her coffee. Now she wanted it black. Probably part of her image as tough and no-nonsense. Well, what was his image going to be?

"How about you, son?" Silverman asked, deliberately condescending.

"Gee I don't know, Dad. How about a soda pop?"

Silverman paused, unsure how to respond. Alex grinned and Silverman chuckled in return. He left them alone.

"You might do all right at this!" Laura remarked.

Despite her compliment, Alex felt unsure about how he would fit in. He was concerned that he might say or do something that would belittle him in Laura's eyes.

It wasn't that he doubted himself. He'd overcome obstacles and endured pain most of these people couldn't imagine. But he wasn't about to reveal all that to Laura. He wanted to be accepted as a man first—not to be the object of pity or even admiration. He wouldn't allow himself to be regarded as a brave person who'd conquered difficulties. That only led to being set apart. If others, including Laura, wanted to believe he was callow or naive, then so be it. He would reveal the true Alex eventually.

The living room of Larry Porter's home was on two levels. In the lower level, modern, white leather couches and easy chairs were arranged around a huge glass-and-chrome coffee table. Off to one side, on the raised level,

stood an electronic keyboard that was obviously not part
of the regular furnishings.

Larry Porter sat in an easy chair, wearing khaki slacks
and a Hawaiian shirt. Rhoda slumped at one end of a
couch, her belly a desk for her steno pad. A rail-thin
young man in perfectly pressed slacks and a starched
white shirt sat beside her. Laura introduced him as Jerry
Deere, and it was a moment or two before Alex realized
she hadn't said "dear." Deere was the head copywriter
for the Universal project. Also present was Mike D'Angelo, Laura's assistant, who was slightly older than Alex.

D'Angelo was talking to Rhoda about his own two
children. When Alex and Laura appeared, conversation
stopped.

"Laura." Larry greeted her with a wave of his hand.
"Come in quick. Mike's getting ready to tell us about his
kids again."

"Better than you starting in about your boat, Larry."
Laura went in and squeezed his hand. "Hi, everyone," she
said, turning to each in turn. "Meet Alex Shaw, musician."

"Hello, Alex Shaw, musician." Deere rose to shake his
hand.

"We met in passing," D'Angelo responded.

"What do you say we do some work?" Larry urged as
Silverman returned with drinks for Laura and Alex.

Within seconds Alex watched the group turn serious.
For nearly two hours ideas were fired around the room.
It gave Alex some fascinating insight into how products
and ideas were sold. There was talk of hard sell and soft
sell; of product collateral, name recognition, and nar-
rowcasting; of points of sale and special-events tie-ins.
Much of the conversation was incomprehensible at first,

but by listening carefully, Alex was able to understand the jargon.

It became clear that there were two main camps. On Larry's side were Silverman and Deere, ready to try and give Gordy just what he wanted. Only D'Angelo and Rhoda stood with Laura, arguing that the idea was impossible.

"Three dozen products, three dozen TV spots, minimum—all unified by a visual and musical theme that is identifiable yet doesn't get in the way of the pitch?" Laura had repeated the same thing six times. "Besides, what makes Gordy think it's a good idea to tie all their products together? Look at Proctor & Gamble. They make about half the brands of detergent that are on the market. But it serves no purpose for them to point that out. It would simply give consumers the impression that all detergents are the same." She leaned back into the leather couch, a look of absolute determination on her face that Alex found sexy.

"Yes," Silverman countered, "but Universal isn't in quite the same position. They don't have that kind of redundancy."

"No, but they make floor wax and frozen TV dinners," Laura insisted. "Do we really want people going to the grocery store to buy a Salisbury steak and suddenly be thinking about floor wax?"

"Yes," Alex said. As all eyes turned toward him, he swiftly regretted opening his mouth. "Umm, sorry. I didn't mean to interrupt."

"No, not at all. I'm interested in getting your input. Why you said yes," Larry prodded.

Alex shot a glance at Laura, who did not look particularly happy with him. "I don't know anything about advertising," Alex hedged.

"Who does?" Deere interrupted sardonically.

"But," Alex continued, "it just seemed to me that since the TV dinners and the wax are all purchased in the same store, why not have someone grab the Salisbury steak and think, 'Oh, should I buy the floor wax, too?'"

He looked over at Laura and winced. She was giving him a withering stare.

Larry pounced. "Aha! Exactly. Why not have them remembering our entire product line as they go aisle to aisle?"

"Because the technical difficulties in this remain overwhelming. Just how are we going to tie all these products together visually? Come up with some kind of cartoon pixie that flits from commercial to commercial saying, 'Another fine product from Universal'?"

Now it was Laura's turn to be stared at.

"That's a *hell* of an idea," Larry said softly.

"I was just kidding, for crying out loud," she protested, rolling her eyes heavenward.

"Kind of a Mickey Mouse sort of deal," added Deere.

"Or like Tinker Bell," D'Angelo interjected.

"Why not one of the Teenage Mutant Ninja Turtles while we're at it?" Laura demanded sarcastically.

"You know, Laura—" Larry pointed a finger at her "—even when you're fighting an idea, you're great. It's perfect. Get the art department working on an elf or a fairy or whatever the hell. And Jerry—" he looked at Deere "—your people come up with a good tag line and a name for the fairy."

"Like the Universal Imp?" Deere suggested.

"Work on it," Larry told him. "So much for the visual unification, Laura. Good job."

"Thanks," Laura muttered bleakly.

"Now, let's talk about the music." Larry looked at Alex. "What do you have in mind?"

"Actually," Alex began cautiously, "I've already written something. It's built around a fairly simple theme—just six notes. But the opening of Beethoven's Fifth Symphony has only those four notes—da-da-da-dum—and everyone recognizes them. So...well, I should play it for you."

Larry nodded toward the electronic keyboard as if to say "Be my guest," and Alex made his way over to it. He turned on the switch and let the instrument warm up a bit.

"First, let me give you the theme—the six notes." He played them at a jaunty tempo. "That's the basic. From that you can make this." He began playing a revised version of the strangely affecting piece he'd played for Laura in her apartment.

"That's kind of the long version, maybe for a more serious product."

"Or a corporate-image ad," D'Angelo said thoughtfully.

"But," Alex continued, "you can also do it this way." He demonstrated a light, humorous air that was identifiably built on the same six notes, but conveyed an entirely different mood. "Or, there's this, a kind of sensual variation." He played yet another version. "Or *this*, with a different rhythm, more rock and roll. Or, here's a kind of bluesy rendition."

Alex deliberately avoided looking at his audience as he played. He was confident of his musical abilities, but this was a different kind of project. These were people, after all, who thought the Yum-Yums jingle was pure genius.

"That's about all I've got, so far," he told them, looking up at last. "I don't know if it's of any use to you. I mean, I've never done anything like this before, and, well..." He trailed off miserably. No one had said a word.

Finally, Larry spoke. "Laura, get this man under contract quick—before he figures out how much to charge us."

WHEN THE MEETING broke up, Laura went to the room overlooking the pool that Larry had set aside for her. Alex had been cornered by Jerry Deere for the moment. And she was glad to get away from him for a while.

Her resistance to Gordy's great vision had been defeated, first by her own big mouth, and then, even more decisively, by Alex's virtuoso performance. How had he done it? It had been just seventy-two hours since he'd come up with a little ditty about a bagel. Now he had a compelling theme with at least five distinctive variations, each damn near perfect. And if there were commercials to be done where no music was called for, they could still use that six-note theme at the end.

She couldn't argue any longer that what Gordy wanted was impossible, because in virtually no time, Alex had gone out and *done* the impossible.

Alex probably didn't realize it yet, but he had, in one instant, become the hottest musician on Madison Avenue. If they got the Universal account, and his music worked as she knew it would, he wouldn't have to worry about playing in seedy blues clubs ever again. The advertising business would take him to its bosom, and a year from now this charming, somewhat reserved, somewhat serious young man would be yet another success story.

And for the foreseeable future, he would be around. He'd invaded her world and become a part of it. And how exactly did she feel about that fact?

She wasn't at all sure.

LUNCH CAME AND WENT uneventfully and by the afternoon work session, Laura had surrendered all opposition and was taking the lead on working out specific job assignments and deadlines. Work was suspended when the sun went down, and the group relaxed with drinks by the pool while Larry insisted on starting the charcoal in his barbecue. Larry's wife Ginger, a gorgeous, leggy blonde, also joined the group, wearing a string bikini that finally silenced Mike D'Angelo on the topic of his wife and children.

"Thank God she doesn't have a brain," Rhoda remarked. Groaning as she rested her feet, she settled heavily into a chaise longue beside Laura.

"She doesn't need one," Laura said sourly.

"Aren't you going in for a swim?" Rhoda asked. "There's still a little sunlight left and besides, as humid as it is, it will be warm all night."

"Actually, I have my bathing suit on under this sundress, but I'm not going to try and compete with *that*."

"Oh, come on, Laura. You have a great body and you know it."

"Uh-huh. But it's a thirty-five-year-old body, and no thirty-five-year-old body looks good next to a twenty-two-year-old former Miss Aluminum Siding."

From the corner of her eye she saw Alex approaching, wearing tight, low-slung jeans and a dark blue T-shirt. Ginger left her station at the barbecue pit to intercept him.

Laura couldn't be certain, but she could have sworn she saw his jaw drop as Ginger introduced herself. "Great," she muttered.

She turned to Rhoda. "Too bad she's married," she commented caustically. "They'd be perfect for each other. Both the same age and all."

"You really think Alex would be attracted to Ginger?" Rhoda questioned. "Well, okay. Attracted. But want to be with her? No way."

"I notice Larry manages to overlook her failings," Laura remarked sarcastically.

"That's Larry. Alex is a different kind of guy."

"It doesn't matter to me, anyway," Laura stated unconvincingly. "I was just making conversation."

All throughout the dinner of barbecued spareribs and ice-cold beer, Laura remained withdrawn. She silently watched Alex become increasingly comfortable with Larry and Ginger and the others. It was amazing how quickly they came to accept him. Somehow that made her discontented. Could it be that she was jealous—that she wanted him all to herself? No. She didn't feel jealous exactly.

Threatened was more like it.

No matter how she held him off, he was forcing his way into her life—forcing her to think of him, to talk about him.

A wave of melancholy washed over her. After providing the obligatory applause for Larry's barbecue skills, Laura pleaded a headache and went up to her room.

HOURS PASSED and still no prospect of sleep. The luminous dials on her bedside clock read 12:05 a.m. Laura sat in an armchair in her darkened bedroom, watching a re-run of *Saturday Night Live*. She felt antsy and unsettled—the way she did after an all-nighter at the office, high on caffeine and adrenaline.

Exercise. That was it. She'd been sitting all day. Laura peeked out the window and saw that the pool was deserted. Only moonlight lighted the water, gilding it with a milky sheen.

She retrieved her bathing suit, a black one-piece with a plunging neckline, and slipped it on. Closing her door softly, she padded down to the pool on bare feet. The night was warm, unseasonably warm for late spring. The moon was nearly full.

Laura made a shallow dive into the deep end, since she couldn't see the bottom. The rush of cool water instantly revived her spirits. She should have thought of this hours ago.

After four laps, Laura rolled onto her back to float. She spent several minutes suspended weightlessly in the water, attempting to identify the constellations of stars overhead.

"Hi, Laura."

She turned her head and saw Alex standing there, hands on his hips, wearing nothing but a small, European-style bathing suit. In the starlight it was very easy to imagine that he was wearing nothing at all.

Laura exhaled slowly, forgetting to breathe, and the loss of buoyancy caused her to sink below the surface. She fought her way back up, spluttering.

"Mind if I join you?" he asked nonchalantly.

Yes, she minded very much. But how could she begin to explain why?

"Suit yourself," Laura answered coolly. She had a bad feeling about this. A very bad feeling that felt . . . good.

Alex dived in smoothly, barely rippling the water. A few seconds later he surfaced behind her.

"Warmer than I expected," he remarked.

"Yes, it's heated."

"I missed you after dinner. I looked over and you were gone."

"Well, I had a headache," she said. The excuse sounded pretty lame.

"Better now?"

"Hmm-hmm." He was drawing slowly closer with each effortless stroke. She could see the thick muscles of his upper arms, water-slick and glistening.

"Did I do okay at the meetings today?"

From his half smile, Laura could not escape the feeling that Alex didn't really give a damn *how* she answered his question. He clearly had other things on his mind.

"You did very well." She couldn't entirely keep the petulant tone out of her voice. "Everyone seems to like you. Larry, Mike, Jerry... Ginger."

"Yeah. I thought so, but I'm never entirely sure. Sometimes I don't read people very well."

"You were close enough to Ginger to read the fine print." *Damn, she hadn't meant to say that.*

"Ginger?" Suddenly he got it. "You're jealous? Of Ginger?" He smiled with satisfaction.

"Jealous? Don't be ridiculous. Just because she's twenty-two, stunning, and married to a man who would cut off both his arms for her?"

"She is pretty."

"Oh. So you noticed?"

"Hard not to." Alex grinned. "But the funny thing is, all she could talk about was how envious she was of you."

"Oh, *please*."

"No, really." Alex grabbed the edge of the pool and pulled closer. "See, Ginger knows what she is—and what she isn't. She's envious of women who have meaningful careers they love. She's bright enough to know she's not the intellectual equal of someone like you, or of some of the other women her husband works with. And she knows that you think she's a bimbo and Larry's an old fool for marrying her."

"She said all this to you?" Laura inquired in disbelief.

"She's very open, if you give her a chance. But she's not resentful of you all for dismissing her. It's kind of sad, but she expects it. She knows all she has is her body...and her love for Larry." Alex shook his head faintly. "To Ginger, you're like some kind of superwoman—beautiful, smart, self-assured and independent."

"Great." Laura sighed loudly. "Now I feel lousy."

"Don't. Just invite her to lunch sometime. She may not be a NASA scientist, but she's a good person."

"And you say you don't read people too well, huh?" Five minutes with Ginger and he had her psychoanalyzed. Come to think of it, he'd done the same thing with Larry. What was Alex's secret? Could he read her with the same ease? She hoped not. "How'd you get so ... so wise at your age?"

Alex laughed softly. He was close by her now, his features hidden in shadow, only a dark outline framed against moon-silvered water.

"My age? How old am I? Am I really the same age as Ginger? Am I really only half as old as Larry? I've lived years that should count for five. Maybe I'm even older than you." He was inches from her now, and with one move he had her trapped. "Maybe it's time you stopped using age as an excuse."

Underwater she felt him press himself to her. Her body went rigid and he eased even closer, cupping the soft curve of her bottom with one hand to keep her afloat.

"Laura," he whispered huskily, trailing warm feathery kisses down the length of her neck. "Relax."

She did, just a little, and he entwined his legs with hers. His hardness, barely contained by thin cloth, grazed her thighs. She let him hold her then, lulled by the cradle of water lapping at her shoulders, dizzy with her own desire. His fingers stroked her cheeks with lazy pressure; his breath was warm and sweet and tantalizingly close.

And then he was there, kissing her with a naked longing so pure, so needy, that nothing else mattered. Denial was out of the question. His tongue dipped and tasted, greedy and insistent, and she couldn't get enough of it.

She was nothing but need. Surrender was going to be so easy now.

His hand rose toward her breast and she sloughed off the strap of her bathing suit so he could peel down the fabric. With her own hand she raked his chest, flattening her palm to feel the hard, urgent beat of his heart, then sliding down over the light dusting of hair, down over the washboard muscles of his abdomen, down—

"Who's down there?" Larry's voice pierced her fog of desire. "Is someone down there?"

She looked up and saw Larry waddling toward the pool, dressed only in a bathrobe.

Fortunately, Laura was at her best in a crisis. She plastered a serene smile on her face, grabbed Alex's head and pushed him under the water.

"It's just me, Larry," she called out. Alex struggled for a moment, but she held firm.

"Oh, Laura. Couldn't sleep?"

"No. I needed some exercise."

Larry was within a few feet of the pool's edge, but that wasn't what worried her. Both straps of her bathing suit had slipped down over her arms, and if Alex had stopped struggling, it was for a very good reason.

"I thought everything went pretty well today," Larry said, making casual conversation.

Laura felt a hand, moving with dreamy slowness in the black water, slide over her naked breast. She shivered visibly.

"Yes," she gasped. "Things went just fine." Alex's touch grew more bold.

"You all right, Laura?" Larry asked with concern.

"Fine, yes. Just a little—" Alex's mouth had joined the fun "—winded." The word came out in a gasp.

Lord, this was torture!

"Oh. Okay. Well, see you in the morning. Can you stay for another day?"

"Uh...uh...no," she managed, on the verge of screaming. "Going to see my mother. Mother's Day." She would never forgive Alex for this.

"Oh, right. Thanks for reminding me. I would have forgotten to call my mother. No point in feeling guilty for a whole year. Well, good night."

"Good night, Larry," Laura said with relief. As soon as he was safely out of sight she released her hold on Alex.

He popped to the surface, gasping for air as he raked back his wet hair with one hand.

"What the hell do you think you were doing?" Laura snapped.

Alex looked at her as though he'd been slapped, but he recovered his composure quickly. "I was fondling your breasts," he explained matter-of-factly.

"You were—" Laura spluttered. "What gave you the idea?"

"You did," Alex shot back. "When you shoved me underwater. Surely you wouldn't do that because you were embarrassed to be seen kissing me. Isn't that right? So, rather than feel insulted and belittled, like I was someone you were ashamed of, well—" his lips formed an ironic half smile "—I felt your breasts, Laura."

He pulled himself up out of the pool in one quick, fluid motion, then turned back to look down at her. Even in the faint light, Laura could see the clear evidence of his rather powerful arousal.

"And let me tell you something, Laura," he said in a voice that had lost all hint of youthful uncertainty. "Tomorrow you can pretend that this never happened, just like you pretend our first kiss never happened. But remember this: I don't lack for willpower. And I don't lack for persistence. So go ahead and deny your feelings. It doesn't matter, because it will happen, Laura." He smiled at her coolly, repeating softly, "It will happen."

He turned and walked away, slowly mounting the steps to his room.

Laura suddenly felt the chill of the water on her skin, but inside she seethed with anger. She pounded the water with her fist. The gall of the man! The unbridled gall of the man! As though he could presume to know what she wanted. Hell, *she* didn't know what she wanted!

Laura also registered the fact she had begun to think of Alex as a man. The prefix *young* had disappeared.

5

LAURA SAT in the Jaguar, listening to its engine hum. The temptation to pull out of Larry's driveway and disappear into the wide-open spaces of Interstate 95 was enormous. The car was packed, the day was young, and on a Sunday morning the highway would be nearly deserted.

She'd had an early breakfast with Larry and Mike. They'd arranged for a dawn tennis match—a frightening exercise in male bonding, if you asked her. Even Laura, who was used to early hours, found tennis at six-thirty in the morning excessive.

Laura had her own motives for dragging out of bed on the one day of the week she traditionally reserved for sleeping in. For one thing, she hadn't had much choice in the matter. She'd spent all night tossing restlessly. And when she finally did fall into an unsettled sleep, she'd dreamed she was submerged and underwater, struggling desperately for air. Above her a hand—a man's hand—was just visible in the murky depths, but every time she went to grasp it, the fingers slipped just out of her reach.

She awakened bathed in sweat, hopelessly tangled in the designer sheets Ginger had ordered for all the guest rooms. It didn't take a genius to figure out what *that* dream was all about. She had to look no further than her encounter with Alex in the pool to come up with enough raw material for a hundred dreams. Even now, when she recalled how she'd felt, weightless and fluid in Alex's hands, her body grew tingly, pulsing with energy....

Fortunately Alex was still asleep, and if she made her getaway now, she wouldn't have to relive the embarrassing moments they'd spent together in the pool. This morning Larry had been his usual jovial self, as if nothing strange had happened the previous evening. She wondered if he was just being discreet, or if her bizarre behavior hadn't registered. With Larry, it was awfully hard to tell.

She'd said her goodbyes and left Ginger a thank-you note, suggesting they get together for lunch sometime, and excusing herself with the more-or-less honest story that she had to stop by her parents' home in Bridgeport. It was Mother's Day. She'd already sent her mother a gift and a card, but she really hadn't seen them in ages.

There was nothing to keep her from shifting into reverse and hightailing it out of there. She knew Rhoda or Jerry would give Alex a lift back to the city, so that wasn't a problem.

Laura glanced up at the bedroom window where Alex was staying, fingering the gearshift with her right hand. What was she waiting for?

Something about this escape by the dawn's early light made her cringe. It wasn't like her to play the coward. When she got herself into an awkward situation with a client or a friend, she confronted the problem head-on. Clear The Air And Get On With It—that was her motto.

But Alex wasn't a client. He wasn't exactly a friend, either.

She depressed the clutch. "Wimp," she muttered as she eased out of Larry's gravel-covered driveway.

She'd traveled a hundred feet down the tree-lined lane when she noticed a steady *crunch, crunch* behind her. A

glance in her rearview mirror confirmed her fears. There
was Alex, running toward her, dressed only in jeans and
a pair of Nikes.

Reluctantly she braked.

Seconds later, Alex appeared at her window, panting
lightly.

"I thought I had a round-trip ticket," he said accusingly.

She forced herself to meet his eyes and saw he wasn't
smiling.

"I've got to stop by my parents' on the way home. I
knew Rhoda or Jerry would give you a ride home." Even
to her ears, her excuse sounded feeble.

"So you just up and run like a thief in the night?" Alex
rubbed his eyes, squinting in the bright morning light.

"Alex. It's hardly nighttime."

He propped an elbow on the hood of the car and
leaned down toward her. "I don't know about you, but
I didn't get a whole lot of sleep last night."

"I slept like a baby."

"Sure!" Alex muttered, clearly unconvinced. He
leaned closer. On the surface Laura was her usual cool,
collected, gorgeous self. But the dark circles under her
eyes and the quaver in her voice gave her away. She was
running from him, that much was obvious. And while
he wasn't entirely sure why she was running, he wasn't
about to give up the chase. He liked seeing her worried.
It meant he had reached her last night. It meant *she*
hadn't slept a goddamn wink, either.

"Laura." She was refusing to meet his eyes. As a matter of fact, she seemed to be fixated on his belly button.
All in all, he supposed he shouldn't argue.

"Do you mind?" she said through gritted teeth.

"Mind?"

"If we have to talk, the least you could do is finish dressing."

"What?" If he wasn't mistaken, the woman was actually blushing.

"Your jeans," she seethed.

Alex glanced down and realized that in his haste to catch Laura, he'd forgotten to fasten his jeans. They hung low on his hips, half zipped. "Oh." He smiled endearingly. "Sorry." He zipped them up slowly, fastening deliberately. She was embarrassed enough for both of them, and he enjoyed her discomfort.

"You try dressing in a second and see how much you leave uncovered," Alex defended himself. "Still—thanks for noticing."

"I didn't notice *any*thing," Laura snapped.

"Not even my tattoo?"

"You don't have a tattoo there—"

"Where?"

Laura pounded her head against the headrest in frustration. "Oh, all right, Mr. Shaw. You've made your point, such as it is. I'd love to stay for the rest of the anatomy class, but I've got to get going."

"Right. I'll just get my bag."

"I have to stop by my parents' home, Alex—"

"Well, it's a little soon to be meeting the folks, but, hey—I guess I'm up for it."

"Alex." Laura rubbed her temples. "You don't want to spend the day listening to my mom discuss her gallstones."

"Sure, I do. Can she cook?" Despite Laura's audible sigh, he knew he'd won.

"I'll give you two minutes. Then I'm outta here."

"Three." He couldn't help gloating. "You wouldn't want me to meet Mom and Dad without a shower and a shave, would you?"

"Whatever." Laura waved him off, clearly defeated.

"How about a little caffeine fix first?" He hoped he wasn't pushing his luck. "I was sort of looking forward to fighting with you over who gets the Sunday comics."

"I don't read the comics, Alex."

"That," he said with a tolerant smile, "would explain why you're such a grouch in the morning."

BRIDGEPORT WAS thirty miles up the highway, and for most of that distance, neither of them spoke. Alex had coerced her into a pit stop at a convenience store for doughnuts, coffee and the Sunday papers, and after that he was seemingly too preoccupied to harass her further.

Laura was furious with herself for letting things go this far. Whatever obligation she felt toward Alex as a co-worker did not extend to spending this much time with him. Still, she *had* offered to be his ride this weekend—but that was before they'd discovered the joys of water sports.

Why had she relented and allowed him to come this morning? She hated it when she didn't behave sensibly—not that it happened often.

She took the Bridgeport exit and for the first time, Alex looked up from his paper. "So," he began, glancing out his window with sudden interest, "were you born here?"

"Uh-hmm. My parents are still in the same house I grew up in."

They passed a gaudy billboard. "The Barnum Museum," Alex read aloud. "As in Phineas T.?"

"Yep." Laura nodded as she braked for a light. "He was a mayor of Bridgeport."

Alex chuckled. "Somehow that seems appropriate."

"What?"

"That you were born in the home of The Greatest Show on Earth. Barnum was sort of the original huckster. Seems right for Ms. Ad Whiz, doesn't it?"

"If you're trying to pick a fight with me about the merits of advertising, it's a bit late, since you're already collaborating with the enemy."

"Whoa." Alex held up his hands. "Truce, okay? Guess I hit a raw nerve. Sorry." He turned away, taking in the scenery. "So," he tried again, "tell me about your parents. Any raw nerves there that I should know about?"

"Not unless you bring up the topic of grandchildren." Laura turned left a little more sharply than she'd intended.

"What about them?"

"They don't have any."

"So? Buy 'em a dog."

Laura laughed dryly. "Don't think I haven't offered. I tried to bribe my younger sister Celeste into providing a grandchild, but she's twenty-one and refused to go for it."

Alex leaned toward her, looking dubious. "Your parents actually give you a hard time about this?"

Laura sighed at his naiveté. Alex seemed genuinely surprised that the subject of her marital status was even an issue—when for her, it was rapidly threatening to become the *only* issue in her life.

"Actually, my parents are very subtle about it. They'll drop little hints, like leaving eight-by-ten glossies of their friends' grandchildren around the house."

"Guerrilla warfare, huh?"

"Sure. Pretty soon it'll be the actual kids themselves, in the flesh. My mother's afraid I have no maternal instincts."

"Do you?" Alex asked ingenuously.

"Alex, there's a proper order to these things. Before you have a baby, it's a good idea to round up a mommy *and* a daddy."

"I always knew we were good for something."

Laura fell silent. She was in no mood to dredge up these tired issues—especially when she could count on her family to do it for her. And it was depressing to see how alien all this was for Alex. It wasn't just the fact that he was young. It was also that he was male. Men could have children *any*time. They weren't forced by Mother Nature to make choices when they weren't ready. They didn't know the terrible fear that came with making irrevocable decisions. It wasn't fair.

"It's all so much easier for you," she muttered, more to herself than to Alex.

"For me?" Alex asked. "Now, what have I done?"

"For you males, I mean."

"Hey, I'm not taking the rap for the entire sex." He slouched back in a bucket seat, pressing his knees against the dashboard.

He stared off into space for a while. "You're right," he said at last. "It is harder for women. In a lot of ways. You have all these options, but you have to juggle them in ways your mothers never had to deal with. It's tough. Of course, it's always a very exciting time for you."

Laura slowed the Jag as she entered a middle-class residential area sporting well-tended lawns and wicker porch furniture. "Why, Alex," she murmured, "I do believe you're *actually* an enlightened male."

"Yeah." He touched her shoulder lightly. "I gave up walking on my knuckles years ago."

Laura pulled in front of a two-story red-brick Colonial. A climbing rosebush threatened to curtain the porch from view. The walkway was lined with long beds over-flowing with spring flowers.

Laura set the parking brake and removed her sunglasses. She felt apprehensive, but wasn't quite sure why. Maybe it was the third degree she anticipated receiving from her mother.

She glanced over at Alex and wondered how he would look in her mother's eyes. "Mention my mother's irises," she said. "You'll have a friend for life," she advised.

"Why? What color are her eyes?"

"The flowers, Alex."

"Ah." He nodded seriously, and she realized he was teasing, trying to get her to relax. "I've got a better idea for your mom. How about we tell her we're getting engaged?"

"Alex!"

"Top that for a Mother's Day gift."

"I think I'll stick with Hallmark."

MRS. DANIELS opened the door even before Laura had reached it. "Honey!" she exclaimed, scooping Laura into a hug. "What a wonderful surprise!" She was tall and slender like her daughter, with short, frosted blond hair and large gold hoop earrings dangling from her ears.

"Hello," she greeted Alex warmly, extending a hand to him. "I'm Karen Daniels."

"Alex Shaw."

Laura caught the unspoken question in her mother's light blue eyes but refused to acknowledge it. *Please, Mom*, she pleaded silently, *don't make this any more awkward than it has to be.*

"Well, come in, come in," Mrs. Daniels said, holding open the door as she led them into the comfortable antique-filled living room. "Sit down, please." She directed Alex toward a Victorian love seat.

Instinctively, Laura gravitated to a chair several feet away.

"What a wonderful surprise," her mother repeated enthusiastically.

"I hope we're not interrupting anything," Laura offered, knowing what her mother's response would be. "I should have called, but this visit was a spur-of-the-moment decision."

"Don't be silly, dear! Your father and I don't have a thing planned. In fact, Daddy's been in back all morning working on the lawn. Right now he and our new neighbor are having it out over who's responsible for trimming the evergreen hedge." She smiled graciously at Alex. "How long can you and . . . your friend . . . stay?"

Alex shifted uncomfortably. Apparently the question was directed at him. "As long as you can stand us?" he ventured.

"Just a little while, Mom," Laura broke in, giving her mother a meaningful look. "Alex and I have to get back to the city this afternoon."

"Well, you can certainly stay for lunch, can't you, Alex?" Mrs. Daniels asked, bypassing her daughter.

"Only if you'll let us do the cleanup," Alex responded.

Great! Laura fumed. *Suddenly he's every mother's dream date.*

"It's a deal." Mrs. Daniels clapped her hands together. "Laura, where did you find this gem?"

"In a deli next to the beef tongue," Laura mumbled.

"Just let me go round up your father," her mother continued, unfazed. "You two stay put."

She went into the kitchen.

"Great, Alex." Laura slumped in her chair. "What do you do for an encore? Walk on water?"

"I was just trying to be helpful." He gave her an irritatingly boyish grin. "You know, I think she likes me."

"With my mother, you're in the son-in-law derby if you have no criminal record and a Y chromosome."

"Well, well. The prodigal daughter returns."

"Daddy!" Laura leaped up to give her father a hug. He was tall and graying, with a thick salt-and-pepper mustache and an authoritative voice that reverberated in the spacious living room.

Alex stood and extended his hand.

"Daddy, this is Alex Shaw. He's a business associate of mine," Laura explained.

"How do you do, sir?"

Mrs. Daniels returned, carrying a tray of glasses filled with iced tea.

"So you're with Tate and O'Neill?" Mr. Daniels asked as the group took their seats and Laura's mother served the tea.

"Temporarily. I'm just scab labor."

"Alex is a free-lancer, Dad," Laura interjected. "He's working up a jingle concept for the Universal Foods account we've been romancing."

"Then you're a musician, dear?" Mrs. Daniels asked, looking disappointed.

"Thank you," Alex said, accepting a frosted glass. "Yes, I am. I play piano at a place in the Village. Mickey-O's."

Mr. Daniels slapped his hand on his knee. "Why, some thirty years ago or so, I used to be a regular there. That was my place to howl, watching Goodman and Brubeck . . . you name it. All the big acts."

"Daddy's a real jazz fan," Laura explained. She could see which way *this* was heading.

"I've got some recordings of Duke Ellington you might enjoy," her father continued. "I mean, these albums are priceless. Karen keeps trying to get me to throw them out, but I stand my ground. Say, maybe you'd like to listen to one."

"Would I!" Alex jumped up from the couch. "You know, they've done some recordings onto CDs of some of the vintage stuff. You'd swear you were in the room."

"Excuse us, ladies." Mr. Daniels stood, and the two men headed for the hallway. "We've got some serious listening to do. Call us for lunch?"

"Run along, boys." Mrs. Daniels waved them off.

Laura pouted, then began sipping at her tea. It was worse than she'd feared; even her father liked Alex.

"Such a nice boy," her mother remarked when the men were safely out of earshot. "And so handsome." She pulled her chair close to Laura's, adding conspiratorially: "I phoned your sister and invited her to lunch."

"Celeste?" Laura exclaimed, pleased. It had been months since she'd seen her sister, who had just started grad school in nutrition. "How's she been?"

"Well, you know, she's locked up in that little lab all day. I don't think she's had a date in ages. She spends every waking minute surrounded by obese rats. Speaking of which—" Mrs. Daniels couldn't resist a sly grin "—how's your love life? Or am I prying?"

"Of course, you're prying." Laura reached over and patted her mother's knee affectionately. "What are mothers for?"

"Did you meet with that matchmaker woman yet?"

"Personal introduction consultant, Mother. And yes, I did. And yes, I liked her. And yes, she liked me. She'll be setting me up any day now with my first date."

Mrs. Daniels chewed on her bottom lip. "I don't know, dear. It all sounds so...so unromantic. Paying this stranger your hard-earned money to find a husband. I guess I prefer the old-fashioned way."

"What exactly *is* the old-fashioned way, Mom? Marry your date from the senior prom and move to a trailer park in New Jersey?"

"Goodness no, Laura. But love is like—" her eyes grew misty "—like spontaneous combustion. It just *happens*."

Where had she heard that tired cliché before? Alex and her mother ought to get together and compare notes. "Mother," Laura chided in exasperation.

"Don't forget how your father and I met. I was at the Bowl-a-Rama with your aunt Jenny. Your father saw how I kept throwing gutter balls and he came over to give me some pointers and...sparks flew."

"It's a wonderful story, Mom. But I don't bowl."

"Well, maybe you should learn." She opened her mouth to continue, but a soft knock at the front door interrupted.

"Celeste, already?" Laura asked. "That girl drives faster than *I* do."

"Laura Lynn Daniels!" her mother hissed as she rose from her chair. "Celeste is a *much* more sensible driver than her older sister, you'll be pleased to hear. I wish to God you'd buy a nice practical car like her little Chevy, instead of that Leopard or Cheetah or whatever it's called."

"Jaguar, Mom."

The knocking grew louder. "That's Hugh Fenton, our next-door neighbor. Doctor Fenton. He's a dentist." Her smile at Laura was positively angelic. "A divorced dentist."

"Mother!"

"Now, Laura. He just happened to be out back when I went to tell your father you'd arrived with your little friend. Daddy borrowed his Weed-Whacker, dear. I was just being neighborly."

"I thought you disapproved of matchmaking," Laura grumbled.

"Only when it's for profit. Try to keep an open mind, Laura." She strode purposefully toward the door, adding over her shoulder: "And just think of all the free dental work."

While her mother played welcoming committee in the hallway, Laura began dreaming up excuses for a quick exit. A migraine? Too conventional. Work? No, that would just invite more parental critiques of her workaholic life-style. Perhaps she could use Alex as an excuse. Pretend he had a gig tonight—or a curfew.

"Laura, dear, this is Dr. Fenton."

Laura reluctantly looked up to see a tall, thin, surprisingly attractive man extending his hand. He was fortyish, with a black beard peppered with gray, steel-rimmed glasses, and very white teeth.

Well, well. She was going to have to change dentists.

"Hugh," he corrected, shaking her hand firmly.

"Please sit," Mrs. Daniels told him. "Duty calls in the kitchen."

Fenton sat down stiffly in a chair across from Laura.

"Mom, let me help—"

"You entertain Dr. Fenton, dear. I'll be a minute." She disappeared into the hallway.

"Would you care for some iced tea?" Laura offered, wishing that her mother hadn't abandoned her so abruptly.

"Never touch the stuff," Fenton replied, adding, "Tannin."

"I beg your pardon?"

"Tannin. Stains the teeth."

"Oh." She nodded. "Does that apply to coffee, too?"

"Absolutely." He smiled widely.

She had to admit his teeth *were* white. Definitely very white.

"Plus, there's the caffeine to be considered."

"What about it?"

"Well, it's a *stimulant*."

"Thank God for that," Laura joked.

Fenton removed his glasses and began cleaning them with a handkerchief he'd pulled from his breast pocket. "Really, it's nothing to joke about. Excessive intake can lead to rapid or irregular heartbeat, irritability, insomnia . . . not to mention dependency."

"Tell me about it."

Fenton looked up from his lens cleaning. There were two red spots on the bridge of his nose where his glasses had perched. "Do you have a problem with caffeine addiction?"

Laura flashed to the drive that morning with Alex. Between them they must have consumed a gallon of coffee. "Well, it's not a problem, exactly. I prefer to think of it as a relatively harmless vice." She smiled politely.

"Which vice is that, Laura?" Alex sauntered into the room, a record album under his arm. Her father was close behind him.

Reinforcements. She sagged with relief. "Coffee," she answered, signaling Alex to join her on the couch.

"Oh." He paused for effect. "Figured you meant the *other* one."

She was too glad to see him to be annoyed. "Alex Shaw. This is Dr. Hugh Fenton."

"Hello," Alex said, shaking Fenton's hand a bit hesitantly. "What kind of doctor, exactly?"

"Hugh's a dentist," Laura volunteered.

"Oh." Alex looked relieved. He settled next to Laura on the couch.

"An endodontist, actually," Hugh corrected.

"Did both my root canals," Laura's father spoke up. "Hurt like holy hell, too." He shook his head, a pained expression on his face, and wandered off toward the kitchen.

Then the front door flew open and Celeste appeared. "Hey, everybody!" she called. Rushing into the living room, she gave Laura an affectionate hug.

"Hi, kid," Laura greeted. "Long time no see. You look great." And she did, too. Celeste looked older and more confident than Laura remembered. She was shorter than Laura and curvier, with long, wavy brown hair and deep blue eyes.

"No, I don't. I'm a blimp," Celeste countered, her pale cheeks blossoming with color. "I live on cupcakes and diet cola at the lab."

"Isn't that what you're supposed to feed the rats?" Laura joked. "Besides, you look just *perfect*." She knew that Celeste, who was shy, sometimes felt eclipsed by her more aggressive big sister. Laura always bent over backward to make her feel comfortable.

"Celeste. I want you to meet Alex Shaw. He's a musician doing some free-lance work with my company."

"Hi, Alex." She extended her hand self-consciously.

"So you're Laura Daniels's sister," Alex murmured, taking her hand in his for what was definitely a longer-than-necessary handshake. "I'll bet you can tell me all kinds of embarrassing things about ol' Laura." He raised his brows suggestively. "Say, like where do you folks keep the high school yearbooks stashed?"

His eyes dropped for just a moment to take in Celeste's rather obvious endowments, and "ol' Laura" gritted her teeth.

"Oh, I'd never betray my sister like that," Celeste told Alex with a smile. "'Course, I suppose her junior high yearbooks are fair game—"

"Celeste!" Laura gasped. "Don't you dare!"

"Her eighth-grade picture she's wearing these huge earrings with peace symbols on them," Celeste whispered to Alex. "She even has this little daisy painted on her cheek."

"Heavy," Alex deadpanned.

"That was the height of the antiwar movement, Alex," Laura explained defensively. "You know what it was like—"

"No, I was just switching to solid food around then."

Laura laughed, but his careless comment made her realize just how many years separated them. She remembered bell-bottoms and the Beatles debuting on *Ed Sullivan*. She remembered a time when envelopes were addressed to "Miss" instead of "Ms."

"I'm often jealous of Laura," Celeste said. "She was there when history was being made. Things I learned about in high school, like hippies and Vietnam . . ."

"Civil rights," Alex added. "The moon landing—"

"Don't forget George Washington crossing the Delaware," Laura broke in sarcastically.

"No. Now I'm not joking, Laura," her sister replied earnestly. "So much was going on in your day. I mean, what's really happened in Alex's and my generation?"

"I don't know. The invention of microwave ovens? Rap?" *Their* generation, Laura thought, beginning to hum the song from The Who, "My Generation."

A few minutes later, her father's shouted invitation to "come and get it" snapped her out of a reverie. Alex and Celeste had gone on talking pleasantly. She caught the tail end of Celeste's whispered explanation that, "She's always done that. Ever since we were kids. All of a sudden she'll be off humming some song that's popped into her head."

"I noticed," Alex answered. "I think that's what's responsible for my introduction to the exciting world of advertising."

The group moved into the dining room. Alex and Celeste continued to carry on their private conversation. Laura watched as Alex leaned toward her sister as though confiding something. Celeste laughed appreciatively, touching Alex on the shoulder.

From her vantage point at the foot of the oval table, Mrs. Daniels was watching, clearly pleased by what was going on.

Something uncomfortable gnawed in Laura's chest—a dangerous feeling that she preferred to regard as hunger. Jealousy was out of the question.

She sneaked a look at Alex. *His* eyes were riveted on Celeste.

"Laura, dear, I thought you and Hugh could sit next to each other over there." Mrs. Daniels pointed to the far side of the dining-room table. "Celeste, we'll put you here—" she guided her toward a chair with all the care of a Broadway choreographer "—and Alex, you sit right next to Celeste, there."

Suddenly Laura realized what must have been painfully obvious to everyone else—her mother was pairing off Alex and Celeste. As if sticking her with Hugh Fenton wasn't enough of a challenge, her mother was going for a double whammy. Two daughters in one afternoon! A matchmaking coup that could put her in direct competition with Margo Morgenroth.

Laura sat woodenly in her chair. What an eye-opener this side trip to her parents' house had become. Sometimes it helped to see yourself through other people's eyes—particularly when you'd deluded yourself into believing the impossible was even remotely possible. How on earth could she even have considered Alex a romantic prospect? Celeste obviously viewed her big sister to be ancient. And her mother thought Hugh Fenton was right up Laura's alley.

There's no fool like an old fool! Well, "old" was a tad melodramatic, but the sentiment seemed awfully appropriate. It wasn't as if she'd ever really believed that she and Alex could get together. She may have fantasized a bit, that's all.

Laura looked up to see Alex carefully studying her from across the table. He cleared his throat and her heart lurched. She was as transparent as crystal, completely readable to him. Alex knew just what she was feeling— like no one else. He would know what to say.

"Would you pass the rolls, Laura?"

There was fantasy, and there was reality. She was going to have to *learn* to tell the difference.

6

"LAURA, I have a confession to make."

"Shut up and breathe, Rhoda." Laura knelt at her secretary's feet, concentrating intently on Julie, their natural-childbirth instructor.

Rhoda propped herself up on her elbows. "It's about Alex."

"Whatever it is, I forgive you," Laura whispered. "Now, can it and concentrate, woman. I'm trying to have a baby here."

"Gee—" Rhoda rolled her eyes "—let me know if I can help."

Laura focused on her stopwatch, biting her tongue to keep from laughing. "Damn it," she cursed under her breath, "you made me lose count again."

"Ladies!" Julie snapped.

Laura winced. *Oh, no. Not again.* They'd already been reprimanded once before for disrupting class when Rhoda told an off-color joke during the pelvic-rocking exercises.

Julie shook her head. Her blond ponytail wagged briskly from side to side and Laura was reminded of a cocker spaniel she'd once owned. "The other couples come in ready to really work," she chastised. "How about you two ladies?"

"Sorry," Rhoda said contritely. "I didn't mean to laugh." She rolled her brown eyes. "Laura made me."

"Rat," Laura muttered.

"That's an important thing for coaches to note," Julie pointed out to the other seven couples spread around the floor. "Laughter can be a marvelous way to release tension. Just remember—" she glared at Laura "—there's a time and a place for everything."

Thoroughly chastened, Laura kept quiet for the rest of the class. It wasn't until she and Rhoda were seated at Dmitri's Café in SoHo, rewarding themselves with their post-class scoop of butter pecan, that Laura recalled her friend's reference to Alex.

"Rhoda," she began suspiciously, "just what was it you were going to confess before Julie so rudely interrupted?"

"No biggie." Rhoda licked her spoon clean. "Besides, you've absolved me."

"Spill it, Rhoda," Laura insisted. "Or I'll tell Julie you're an unwed mother."

Rhoda set down her spoon. "Okay. Anything but that. Julie already thinks I don't work and play well with others. Remember you told me how Alex came over to your place the same evening as Margo the Matchmaker?"

"Yeah. So?"

"Didn't you wonder how he found your place?"

"I dunno. Looked under 'Older Woman' in the yellow pages? I guess I was too preoccupied to give it much thought."

"Well *I* told him." Rhoda smiled serenely as if a great weight had been lifted from her soul. "The day Larry hired him on."

"Rhoda," Laura groaned. *"Why?"*

"Because he asked. *You* try looking into those incredible green eyes and saying no." She cocked her head. "But then, maybe you already have...."

"There's nothing going on between Alex and me," Laura said defiantly.

"Then you *did* say no."

"He didn't ask," Laura lied. She toyed with her napkin. Why was she being so evasive? Rhoda was her friend. "Well, okay, he *did* kind of ask. Sort of."

"Wait a minute." Rhoda held up her hand. "I've lost track. Are we talking about what I think we're talking about?"

"Nothing happened, Rhoda." Since she'd been so embarrassed at her parents' house, Laura couldn't take any more ribbing—no matter how good-natured—about her age. "We kissed. That's all."

"Where?" Rhoda asked.

"The first time at my place, the night he came over." She smiled in spite of herself. "Margo showed up and caught us in flagrante delicto."

"Red-handed, eh?" Rhoda rubbed her palms together gleefully.

"Red-faced. She nearly had a cow. I told her some story about Alex being an old friend from Maryland."

"She bought it?"

"I doubt it, but she was too genteel to press the issue. We went through with the interview like nothing ever happened."

Rhoda spooned up a dollop of ice cream. "So if that was the first time, where was the second?" She frowned. "Wait a minute. Not at *Larry's*?"

Laura smiled in response. Despite her embarrassment, the memory of those moments in the pool with Alex still sent a jolt of longing through her. She reached for her coffee. The soft clatter of cup against saucer warned her that her fingers were trembling.

"Let me guess," Rhoda continued. "That big four-poster bed in your room?"

"Worse."

Rhoda chewed on her tongue, cataloging the possibilities. "The pool table?" she ventured.

"You're getting warmer."

Rhoda gasped audibly. "Why, Ms. Daniels! I didn't know you had it in you. Larry Porter's *pool?*" Laura nodded and Rhoda rolled her eyes. "And I had to go to bed early that night. I always miss all the fun stuff."

"We just kissed," Laura explained patiently. Even as she said the word *kiss*, she could feel Alex's mouth on her breast—liquid heat in the cool stillness of the water. It had not been "just" a kiss. She knew it and Alex knew it, but there was no need for anyone else to know.

"Oh, but Laura...in the moonlight with the water and all. How romantic can you get?" Rhoda's eyes grew misty. "Can you tell I miss Rick?"

"He'll be home soon." Laura gave her a reassuring pat. "Hopefully, just in time to put me out of a coaching job."

"I'm not so sure, the way that exercise in the Mediterranean is going." Rhoda toyed with her wedding band. "So, anyway, finish telling me about your pool party."

"There's nothing to tell. Larry walked in on us."

"Oh, my God! What did you *do?*"

"I nearly drowned Alex, that's what I did. You know Larry. He was oblivious."

"First Margo, then Larry," Rhoda mused. "I'm beginning to detect a pattern here."

"It's just as well." Laura shrugged. "If they hadn't stopped us, I would have."

"Are you so sure about that?" Rhoda's tone was somber now. "Laura, far be it from me to butt into your personal life—"

"I feel a but coming here—"

"*But*, I don't think you're even giving this guy a chance. Here's this gorgeous, intelligent, gifted, sensitive, gorgeous, funny man drooling all over you—"

"Rhoda!"

"Well, you know what I mean. And you won't even give him a chance because you're obsessed with his birth date. Did I mention he was gorgeous?"

Laura leaned forward, cupping her chin in her hand. "A week ago I might have bought that line of reasoning," she said.

"What happened to change your mind?"

"We went to see my parents on the way home from Larry's. Alex and I. My sister Celeste was there—she's a year younger than Alex—and seeing them together I realized there's a huge gulf separating us. A real generation gap."

"Oh, *please!*" Rhoda scoffed.

"No, I'm serious, Rhoda." Laura's voice sounded harsh to her own ears. "There are things that shaped who I am—music and clothes and politics—that Alex will never understand because he wasn't there."

Rhoda remained unconvinced. "Big deal! Rick came from Iowa and I was born in Queens. There's a gap if I ever saw one. And who cares? That's what makes life interesting."

"You don't understand. You had to see them together." Beneath the table Laura clenched and unclenched her fist, trying to squeeze away the tension that was threatening to take command of every major muscle group in her body.

"You're not suggesting Alex was interested in Celeste?"

"How do I know? Why wouldn't he be?"

"Because he's interested in *you*, honey. And the sooner you get that through your head, the sooner you can apply for a refund from that Margo dame."

Laura exhaled slowly, counting to ten. Rhoda was loyal if very misguided. There was no point in prolonging the argument. "You know, your matchmaking instincts are as bad as my mother's."

"We'll see. Have you seen Alex since your parents'?"

"No, thank God. He's been working at home. Says our studio was 'too high-tech' for him. He prefers a real piano. I'll certainly have to see him tomorrow."

"Oh, right. The big presentation to Gordy?"

Laura stared off into space. "Yeah, I guess I'd better get used to seeing Alex around the office—for a while, anyway."

"How about around the 'ol co-op, huh?"

Laura favored her secretary with a conspiratorial smile. "Tell you what. You leave the name Alex out of your conversation for the rest of the evening and I'll buy us both another scoop of butter pecan."

"Forgive me, Alex," Rhoda whispered. She reached for Laura's hand and shook it. "Deal. But only for tonight."

After dropping Rhoda off, Laura arrived home to find her answering machine beckoning with a flashing green light. To her surprise, it was none other than Margo herself.

"Laura, dear, it's Margo Morgenroth. I have wonderful news for you, darling. Believe me, if I weren't happily married... Suffice to say this fellow is Eligible Bachelor of the Decade material. Tall, dark, handsome, plus he's the president of a Wall Street investment firm— and I do mean one of the best. Very intelligent, supersensitive—he writes *poetry*, Laura. A real Renaissance man. Is your machine going to turn off? I despise these contraptions but I just had to let you know the great news. And Laura? Get this—the man *loves* anchovy pizza. Can you believe it? A match made in heaven, I'm telling you. Call me tomorrow, dear. Unless you already have too much on your plate. This one won't last!"

Laura clicked off the machine and flopped onto the rock-solid Creamsicle couch. For a moment she pictured Margo ticking off vital statistics into answering machines all around Manhattan. Was she calling some other woman with a taste for anchovies to set *her* up with the same man?

"This one won't last." Laura giggled. Maybe Alex was right. It did seem a little crude, all this matchmaking stuff. On the surface, of course, Margo had oozed class from every pore. She was a petite woman in her fifties, with gleaming shoulder-length gray hair and a pair of hefty diamond earrings. She'd been no-nonsense and a bit officious, but Laura had found that reassuring at the time. This was serious business. In retrospect, it seemed, well, unromantic.

Still ... Tall, dark, handsome ... She closed her eyes and tried to imagine Mr. Renaissance sitting in his office across the street from the Stock Exchange, chowing down pizza while penning Petrarchan sonnets with his free hand. Somehow the image wouldn't quite gel. What she got instead was a vision of Alex sitting at his piano wearing worn-out jeans and very little else, playing a melody so haunting she got chills imagining it. His apartment was dark, his body glowed in the moonlight, and the song never quite seemed to end....

Hours later she awoke on the couch, softly humming the same melancholy tune. She picked up the phone and ordered a large pizza with anchovies. Surely Renais-

sance men, she reasoned, liked their women on the
plump side.

"SO. IT'S THE BIG DAY." Alex leaned in Laura's office
doorway, wiggling his eyebrows in a parody of anticipation.

Laura's heart surged at the sound of his voice. "About
time," she chided. She didn't want to tell Alex how often
she'd checked her watch in the past hour. "You said you'd
be here with plenty of time to spare and we're supposed
to be on the helipad in five minutes."

"The what?"

"The helipad." Laura grinned, unable to hide her ex-
citement. "We'll be catching a helicopter up on the roof
to fly us all out to Gordy's yacht in the harbor."

"You're kidding."

"We're going to descend on them like birds of prey,
amaze them with our presentation and then disappear
into the sky again—" she waved her hand skyward
"—with a half-billion-dollar account in our pockets."

"Gee, boss, can I sit by the window. Can I? Can I?
Huh?"

"Well, have you done all your homework?"

Alex snapped a military salute. "Music all present and
accounted for. You'll notice that I am wearing my one and
only suit in honor of it all."

Laura had noticed. Alex didn't look nearly as out of
place as she might have expected—or as he probably felt.
As a matter of fact, he looked great. He looked older and
more worldly in his gray pin-striped suit. But the images
of him that stuck in her mind were less...buttoned-down
than this. "You look great," she told him with more feeling than she'd intended.

"Miss me?" he asked, his tone shifting to a more serious plane.

"It's only been a few days since I've seen you." *Actually,* Laura added silently, *I've seen you many times from this very window. Seen you at your piano. Fantasized about you. Dreamed—*

"I know," Alex murmured. "But I've missed you."

"Let's get going," Laura said quickly, glancing ostentatiously at her watch.

At that moment Larry arrived with Barry Silverman in tow. "You all ready?"

It was obvious that Larry was suffering from nerves. "We're ready, coach," Alex said to Larry, adding with mock seriousness, "Let's go out there and kick some butt."

"Rah, rah," Laura offered, standing up to join them.

"Go, team!" Barry joined in.

"Okay, then," Larry replied seriously. "What's the worst that could happen? They'll say no?"

"No, Larry." Laura patted his shoulder. "The worst that could happen is the helicopter slams into the World Trade Center."

"Thanks, Laura. I hadn't thought about that." Barry Silverman rolled his eyes.

The high-speed elevator took the group to the top floor, and from there they climbed four flights of steel stairs to reach the roof. Fifty yards away a green and yellow helicopter was landing on a painted bull's-eye, its rotors chopping the air.

They walked quickly toward the chopper, bending low as they'd seen people do in countless movies, though the rotors were well above their heads.

The pilot, wearing headphones and dark aviator sunglasses, motioned them into the passenger area, which boasted gray airline-style seats. As soon as they were belted in, the pilot raised the RPMs and the helicopter lifted clear of the landing pad and tilted forward.

As the rooftop slid past, Laura found herself staring down at the street, which was quickly followed by the face of a taller building that seemed to be rushing toward them. But the pilot banked sharply, and in less than a minute they were out over the water looking down at a scattering of pleasure craft, and the Staten Island ferry, with its top deck jammed with people.

Almost immediately the helicopter began to lose altitude and, looking ahead over the pilot's shoulder, they could make out a huge yacht. On its rear deck was a painted bull's-eye that looked too small to accommodate the chopper.

When they came gingerly to rest on the deck of the gently rolling yacht, the helicopter's tail extended well out over the water. They disembarked from the noisy craft, hauling huge briefcases and artist's carryalls. Alex had brought a portable electronic keyboard in a leather carrying case.

The helicopter pulled swiftly away, leaving their ears ringing. A white-jacketed crewman stepped forward. "Tate and O'Neill?" Larry nodded and the crewman said, "Follow me, please."

They were given fifteen minutes to set up in a sleek, teak-paneled conference room that—if it weren't for the round portholes—might have been any corporate boardroom in the city.

The presentation was a combination slide show, lecture and concert. They showed Gordy, who'd arrived on the scene wearing a blue blazer, yachting cap and alligator-skin cowboy boots, the computer-animated sequence that had the cartoon fairy, Newt, introducing individual commercials with a wave of her magic wand. They projected storyboards for two specific commercial concepts and listened while Alex played the "Universal Anthem with Variations." Barry Silverman talked about their rough plan of action in terms of media buys, and Larry got up at the end to say that Tate and O'Neill would devote its every waking hour and all its considerable resources to what would become their single biggest client.

When Larry sat down, Gordy looked at him and asked, "Is that it?"

Laura could feel her heart sink as Larry answered dully, "Umm, yes. Of course—"

But Gordy held up a hand, cutting short Larry's ready entreaties. "You're hired, Porter. No contest. The job is yours. Now, let's celebrate."

For a long moment the room was silent. Laura looked at each in turn. Yes, Larry's mouth was open. Barry's, too. And Alex looked equally stunned. Then she realized her own jaw was slack. The four of them sighed and sank back into their chairs.

Appreciating their reaction, Gordy laughed. "Well, when you all come back down to earth, I'll expect you topside for drinks." He left, chuckling.

"Just like that?" Silverman wondered, starting to grin.

"You're hired, Porter," Laura repeated, shaking her head.

"The fifth-biggest account in the country." Larry looked like he'd experienced a divine revelation. "We'll be the third-biggest agency in the U.S. We'll— I gotta make a call."

As Larry opened a briefcase cellular phone, Alex turned to Laura. "Congratulations. I guess that's the right thing to say."

Laura nodded her head as if in a dream. "Yes, it is. Thanks to you in large part."

"I'll second that," Larry chimed in, listening intently to the telephone pressed to his ear. "Mr. O'Neill? Larry Porter." He looked up at his companions, grinning widely, before continuing. "I just wanted to let you know we're going to have to hire fifty or sixty new people. Yes. Yes, sir, the whole ball of wax. Yes, sir, it's ours. Congratulations to you, too, sir. That's right." He glanced up at Laura. "Yes, Laura Daniels."

Laura felt her heart clutch at the sound of her name.

Larry was smiling and nodding his head now. "I would be very happy to tell her. Very happy. Yes, sir. No, we've been invited to stay and have drinks with the client. That would be best. Goodbye."

Larry set the phone back in its cradle and clapped his hands together, rubbing them enthusiastically. "Laura, the big man says, 'Well done.' And he mentioned that there was a partners' meeting next month. He wondered if you might wish to attend."

Laura felt her breathing stop.

"At that meeting," Larry added dramatically, "you'll be offered partnership in Tate and O'Neill."

She closed her eyes and breathed deeply. *Partner!* The first woman to make partner! A position that carried with it an income—between salary, bonuses, stock dividends and profit sharing—of nearly a million dollars a year.

Since leaving college nearly thirteen years earlier, this had been her goal. Now it was very nearly within reach. All she had to do was go into that meeting at the end of the month and say yes.

"Shall we join our client on deck?" Larry suggested.

Out in the fresh air again, Laura noticed that the sun was setting. The yacht rode the gentle swell smoothly, tugging only occasionally at its anchor chain. White-jacketed waiters were handing out martinis, gin-and-tonics and white wine. She took a glass of wine and made small talk with one of Gordy's vice presidents.

Success. And she felt nothing. Probably just numb, Laura reassured herself. Right now, she was just numb. Later there'd be time enough to jump up and down.

"So, partner." Alex appeared before her, eyeing her with curiousity, compassion. "Are you going to take the job?"

How was it that only Alex would have known that *that* was the question? Anyone else would just have assumed as much. Hell, she'd assumed it—right up to the second when it was offered.

"It's what I always wanted," she answered belatedly.

"Mmm-hmm." He sipped at his drink. "I wouldn't presume to offer advice, but there are two things you should think about right now."

"Oh?"

"First. It's a very big thing to get the offer. Enjoy that, in and of itself, before you worry about your answer," he said earnestly.

Laura thought about that for a moment. "You know, Alex, you're dead right. It's a hell of a thing to be offered."

"You should be proud," Alex encouraged her.

"Damn right, I should be. And I am." She laughed suddenly. "All right, now. What was the second thing I should think about?"

In answer, Alex put his arm around her shoulder and turned her to face the city. Lights had begun to appear in the skyscrapers as the sun sank swiftly behind them.

"The second thing you have to think about is this—you have something to celebrate, and right there—" Alex waved expansively to encompass downtown Manhattan "—right there is the biggest, wildest playground on earth. We're young, we're free and we have credit cards in our pockets. So what are we doing moping around here?"

THE GETAWAY WAS EASY.

Laura claimed to have a touch of the flu, and Alex, ever the gentleman, insisted on escorting her back to shore. Gordy assigned a speedboat and one of his crewmen to shuttle them. After the requisite handshakes and expressions of concern, they were on their way.

"I feel like a kid playing hooky," Laura shouted at Alex as they sped toward the marina.

"Enjoy it!" he called back over the noise of the engine.

Once again ashore, Alex hailed a cab and they sped through the New York night, fugitives from responsibility.

MICKEY-O'S was in the heart of Greenwich Village in a basement beneath a row of boutiques. It was cramped and smoky, but even early on a Monday evening the club was filling up rapidly. Alex led Laura inside. While she gazed at the walls covered with jazz memorabilia, he exchanged a few words with the doorman, who couldn't seem to get over the sight of Alex in a suit.

They settled at a little table near the raised platform that served as a stage for the musicians. A red plastic cloth was draped over the tabletop and a little white candle flickered in the middle.

"Believe it or not, they do serve food here," Alex said. "And some of it is almost edible."

"Good, because I'm famished," Laura answered. "You can really work up an appetite getting promoted."

Alex looked pensive.

"What's wrong?" Laura asked.

"Oh, I don't know. It seems like you should be somewhere special tonight." Alex frowned. "You know, dinner at Le Cirque or whatever. Instead I bring you here."

"You forget—this place comes highly recommended. My dad was quite impressed that you play here. He says a lot of the greats started here."

"I liked your dad a lot." Alex smiled. "That Duke Ellington record he gave me is priceless."

"He liked you, too. He wouldn't have given you that record if he didn't. None of my other—" she paused, catching herself before she blurted the word *dates* "—uh, friends, ever rated that kind of tribute."

He looked at her with the maddeningly analytical gaze that she'd come to think of as his "anthropologist's" look. It generally preceded some intensely personal question that, from someone else, might come across as downright rude. From Alex's lips, it would seem perfectly reasonable.

"So?" Laura pressed. "Go ahead and ask me."

"Ask you what?"

"Whatever it is that you were just debating about asking me."

"Damn." Alex grimaced. "Am I that obvious?"

"No. I'm that perceptive."

Alex chuckled. "I was going to ask you how many other . . . *friends* . . . there'd been in your life." He leaned back in the rickety bentwood chair, his arms crossed over his broad chest.

Laura stared back in amazement. "You don't actually expect me to answer that?"

"Why not?"

"*Because*, Alex. Because it's..." She trailed off, studying the ceiling. This was just how she'd felt when he'd asked her about Margo. "You know, Alex..." She tried again. "Sometimes I wonder if you dropped in from another planet."

He shrugged carelessly. "I suppose I have, in a manner of speaking."

"You're just so...so curious. You question everything." Laura looked away. "And then, no matter what I say, you make me doubt myself."

"Does this mean you're not going to tell me?"

She drew in her breath audibly. "I'll tell you when you tell me."

It was Alex's turn to look away. He focused on the far wall, his lips pressed into a grim line.

"Turnabout is fair play," Laura bantered, wondering if perhaps she'd gone too far. Maybe Alex was getting over an unhappy affair. Maybe he was in love with someone now and things weren't working out. For a moment, neither spoke.

At last he broke the tension with a forced grin. "Hey, what am I wasting time with you for? I've got other very reliable sources."

"You mean Celeste?" She surveyed the floor for a waitress. Her mouth was suddenly desert-dry.

"There'll be a waitress around in another hour or two," Alex joked, following her gaze. "And yes, I mean Celeste. That sister of yours has great possibilities."

I told you so, Rhoda, Laura thought with grim satisfaction. "I'll be sure to pass that along to Celeste," she said brittlely.

Alex's eyes clouded. In the smoky dimness of the room, they looked very nearly black. "I meant as a spy," he clarified. "What did you *think* I meant?"

Laura opened her mouth to respond, but before she could say a word, a waitress materialized at her side.

"Alex Shaw! In a suit, no less!" The young girl, who looked as if she'd barely reached the legal drinking age, whistled.

"That's right," Alex whispered theatrically. "You know me as Alex Shaw, destitute piano player. But, when there's money to be made, I turn into Super-Sellout!"

"Oh." The girl nodded with sudden understanding, tossing back a mane of frizzy black hair as she turned to look at Laura. "You must be the ad lady."

"Becky, this is Laura Daniels." Alex made the introductions. "Laura, Becky. Laura," Alex continued, "has just been made a partner in her agency, so we're celebrating. So it's overpriced champagne and generous tips all around."

"Congratulations," Becky said, managing some enthusiasm.

"And some of whatever looks edible in the kitchen," Alex added.

"Are you going to play tonight?" Becky questioned.

"Naw." Alex shook his head. "I'm a bit overdressed."

"Too bad." Becky turned again to Laura. "He's really good."

"I know," Laura answered with cool authority.

The waitress left to pick up their champagne and Laura eyed Alex critically. "Are you and she—?" She let the question hang.

"Becky?" Alex seemed surprised, but recovered quickly. "Laura," he chastised. "You're so curious. Why, you question *everything*...."

"Okay, I can take a hint." But the truth was, she'd begun to realize just how many questions she did want to ask. Alex had been an enigma for too long. Tonight she was going to get to the bottom of Alex Shaw.

"Speaking of questions," she ventured, "you've never told me anything about your family. While you've already met mine."

Alex shifted a little in his chair. "What do you want to know?"

"Do you have any brothers and sisters?"

"Two younger brothers. Pete and Gary. They're both into music, too. Peter plays bass and Gary bangs on the drums a bit. When we were kids my parents used to get us to play as a combo when they had parties. I don't know who it was harder on—us or their guests." He laughed self-deprecatingly.

"Sort of like the Osmonds," Laura offered.

"Who?"

"The— Oh, never mind. They were before your time." She folded her hands on the table. "What about your parents?"

"My dad owns a landscaping business. My mom's a lawyer."

"No kidding?" That seemed strange, somehow, to Laura. But then, any background of Alex's would have seemed strange. She'd had to think of him without any context. As a man without a past.

"Yeah." He smiled slyly at her. "See, I know all about women juggling a family and a career. I'm one of the juggle-ees. And I survived more or less unscathed. Men like me make the best catches, too."

"Oh? How's that?" She couldn't resist returning his flirtatious smile.

"Well, for example, I can cook. Omelets and macaroni. And I know how to separate my whites from my permanent press." He studied her, his eyes glimmering in the candlelight. "Plus I grew up thinking it was okay for a woman to have more than one priority in her life. Strong women, independent women—some men are scared by them."

"Not you, though?" Laura asked softly, mesmerized by the reckless tone in his voice.

"I love a challenge." Alex reached across the table and let the tips of his fingers graze her own.

How could such an innocent whisper of a touch promise so much more? Instinctively Laura pulled her hand away. "Um—" she cleared her throat "—is that why you came to New York? For the challenge?"

Alex leaned forward on the table, resting his chin on his palm. "You know, I can't get enough of that voice of yours," he marveled, ignoring her question. "It's like some intoxicating drug."

"And speaking of intoxication—" Laura interrupted as Becky arrived with the champagne.

"You don't sing, do you, Laura?" Alex pursued. "A voice like that, you should be singing Gershwin. 'Someone to Watch Over Me,' maybe."

The subtle, full curve of his lower lip was hypnotizing. Laura jerked her gaze away and watched Becky open the bottle of Veuve Clicquot.

"How about 'Embraceable You'?" Alex leaned a little closer.

"I only sing in the shower," Laura muttered.

"Better yet. Ever heard 'The Man I Love'?"

"No." Laura smiled sweetly. "But perhaps you've heard of one of my favorites: 'Let's Call the Whole Thing Off'?"

Alex smiled. Further conversation was impossible after a trio of musicians took the stage. There was a brief introduction, then the group launched into a swing composition with an infectious rhythm.

Food arrived in the form of various finger foods, but Alex hardly ate; his eyes were locked on the nearby keyboard player. After a few minutes Alex removed his jacket and rolled up his shirt sleeves. As he loosened his tie, the sway of his body responding to the beat was barely perceptible—even to Laura, who found herself fascinated by the sexiness of his movements.

Her lids began to grow heavy, and she felt lulled by the pure pleasure of the moment. Nothing mattered except the fact that she felt wonderful, here and now. She felt the tension in her shoulders ease. Slowly the music and the champagne took hold of her, forcing her body to move in slow harmony with Alex's.

She let her eyes close, and when the song ended she opened them to find Alex eyeing her boldly. Had any man *ever* looked at her with such need? His face was grave. His youthful arrogance was gone. It wasn't just her body he wanted. It was *her*.

"Folks, do we have a treat in store for you." The silver-haired club manager had stepped up on stage. "One of our rising young stars here at Mickey-O's had the nerve to show up on his day off, and if he thinks he's sneaking out without playing at least one number, he's got another thing coming. Ladies and gentlemen, Alex Shaw!"

The room burst into enthusiastic applause. Apparently Alex had built up quite a following.

He looked at Laura. "Do you mind?"

"Mind? Are you kidding?" Laura laughed. "I can't wait."

"I promise. Just one or two." Alex waved to the audience as he headed to the stage.

A survey of the room told Laura she wasn't the only woman watching Alex intently. One girl in the back of the club even let out a wolf whistle.

Alex cleared his throat and tapped the microphone with his finger. "Thanks, everybody. Sorry about the monkey suit." He looked down at his tie and laughed. "I've been at a masquerade party. I went as Robert Palmer. I'd like to do a piece—a new piece—that I wrote for a very special friend of mine. She's here tonight." He winked at Laura and dozens of heads turned to catch a glimpse of her. "B-flat, boys. Jump in whenever you're ready."

The keyboard player moved to an electronic organ, leaving Alex the piano. A hush settled over the crowd and Laura realized that she, too, was holding her breath. She saw Alex's fingers resting lightly on the ivory keys. His eyes were half closed.

Then it began—a haunting, deceptively simple melody that wrapped itself around her like a tender embrace. The other musicians joined in after a while, improvising delicately while never losing the sweet central theme. Without knowing quite why, Laura began to cry softly.

She reached for a paper napkin and blew her nose. How embarrassing. It wasn't like her to be so sentimental, but something about the piece made her feel vulnerable. It was so beautiful! And it was *hers*.

As the music faded away, the room erupted into emotional applause. Alex turned to look at her. There was a slow trickle of perspiration running down his temple and his face was red. He caught sight of her just as she was dabbing away a tear with her napkin.

Alex said something to the band and they began a bluesy rendition of a song she recognized as "Someone to Watch Over Me." Smiling to herself, she reached for her champagne glass and took a sip.

"You must be the 'very special friend' who inspired our boy Alex." Sitting across from her was the silver-haired man who'd introduced Alex. "Hi, I'm Danny Oransky. I own the club."

"Aren't you 'Mickey'?" Laura asked good-naturedly.

"My great-uncle," Oransky explained. "The original Mickey died in '61. This place has been in existence even longer than I have. And a whole lot longer than you have, young lady."

"Well, it's a great place. My dad used to hang out here when he was a hepcat, or whatever it was in those days."

"Good. That's good." Oransky smiled contentedly as he paused to listen to the music for a moment. Then, shaking his head slowly, he said, "I don't know what you're doing, but keep up the good work. That was a nice tune you seem to have inspired." He leaned closer to be heard above the swelling music. "It makes me feel good to see Alex so happy. Hell of a kid. Hell of a musician, too. One of these days we're going to be bragging over the fact that he started out here. And, man, when you think of all he's been through . . . Boy's got more guts in his little finger..." Oransky paused, taking in a few bars of Gershwin before continuing. "Anyway, like I say, keep inspiring. Whatever you're doing, it's working." Oransky stood slowly and headed toward the service bar.

Laura took a gulp of champagne and rolled Oransky's words around in her head. *"All he's been through... He's got more guts..."* What could Oransky be talking about? She remembered Alex talking about a "bad accident." Or, more accurately, *not* talking about it. And there was that scar she'd seen that day in the weight room at his apartment building. A nasty scar that ran half the length of his spine. She wondered if she should ask him about it directly. If it was too personal, why would someone like Oransky know? Besides, tonight was the night she'd resolved to get a fix on Mr. Alex Shaw, come hell or high water.

The song ended, and after acknowledging the audience's warm applause, Alex returned to the table. "Whew!" He sighed, collapsing into his chair. "It's too hot up there for a long-sleeved shirt and tie, let me tell you." He swigged down half a glass of champagne, raking back his damp hair with his free hand. "So, what did you think?"

His tone was light, but the look in his eyes told her how much her response mattered to him. "I think—" She hesitated. "I think if I live to be a hundred, I'll never receive a more wonderful gift."

Alex nodded and stared down at his fingers, which he was nervously drumming on the tabletop. It was probably the first time she'd ever seen him actually embarrassed. And it was very charming.

"When did you write it?" she asked.

"Late one night last week. I couldn't sleep, and I was looking out over the avenue and there was your office. What better inspiration could a guy ask for?"

"My office?"

"Yeah. You know how it's directly across from my place?"

Did she ever. For a second, Laura considered confessing to her voyeuristic tendencies. Instead she decided to broach the topic Oransky had introduced.

"Alex," she began softly, twirling the stem of her wineglass between her thumb and forefinger, "Danny Oransky stopped by the table."

"He's a good guy. One of the best in a business that has plenty of jerks."

"He mentioned something about . . . your accident."

Alex flinched as though she'd slapped him. "What did he tell you?" Alex demanded.

"Nothing. Nothing at all. I was just wondering."

"What the hell business is it of yours?" The cords in his neck stood out.

"It isn't, really." Laura paused, thrown off balance by the unexpected anger in his voice. But it was too late to retreat. "It's just that you're such a puzzle to me and I thought maybe if I laid my hands on the missing pieces, everything else would fall into place." She dropped her gaze, and saw his hands clenched into white-knuckled fists. "I'm sorry," she whispered.

Alex shoved back his chair and stood abruptly. "Come on. Let's get out of here." He slung his jacket over his shoulder and strode toward the exit. "Put it on my tab," he shouted to Becky. He was out the door before Laura could even stand.

Outside, the air was crisp and still. She found Alex near the curb, trying to hail a cab.

"I thought I had a round-trip ticket," she reminded, touching his shoulder tentatively.

"You do. I just needed some air."

He was erecting a wall between them. She could feel it. If she didn't do something about it quickly, she'd lose any hope of ever reaching him.

The thought terrified her. She stepped in front of him—so close her breasts grazed his chest—and laced her fingers behind his head and pulled him to her, kissing him urgently. Alex gently disengaged himself, his expression a blur of desire and confusion.

"Please," Laura said hoarsely, "don't shut me out, Alex."

He responded by flagging down a cab. He gave the cabbie an address and settled back beside Laura.

She closed her eyes and sighed. She'd had no idea how much she'd wanted to hear those words till he'd spoken them: The address was his own.

The ride was brief, and neither spoke until they reached Alex's apartment. Whatever he had to say, Laura knew she'd have to wait until he was ready.

Alex lit a brass lamp on the piano and a pale yellow fan of light spread across the hardwood floor. "Sit down," he told her. She did as he asked, perching on the edge of the couch.

Alex took off his tie and loosened the top two buttons of his shirt. He paced the small room, his hands folded behind his back. Finally he spoke. He stood directly in front of her, hands on his hips.

"I told you I had an accident."

"Yes," she urged him on gently.

"It was bad. Really bad." There was no trace of humor in his voice. His face had gone gray, and in his eyes was a look of hatred. "I was seventeen. Guy hit me head-on. He crossed the line and hit me. When I woke up . . ." He walked over to the window and blindly stared out. After a few minutes, he turned around and continued. "It's impossible for me to convey the pain, the horror—the goddamned fear." He forced himself to take a breath. He wiped tears from his eyes with the back of his hand. "The fear," he repeated.

"They told my parents I wouldn't make it. That they should prepare themselves for the worst." He smiled bitterly. "As you may have guessed, I survived. Then they told me I'd never walk. I walked. If I took enough drugs to kill the pain, I was too doped up for physical therapy. So I had to live with the pain. I don't ever want to face anything that hard again."

"You told me once you had lived years that counted for five," Laura said softly. "I thought . . ."

"That was no exaggeration. While other kids were learning to drive cars, I was learning how to drive a wheelchair and how to walk with leg braces. After three and a half years, I took my first real step. I told my doctor, 'You son of a bitch, you said I'd never walk. Take a look at this!'" Alex laughed. "He looked at me and said, 'Alex, if you ever want to get a man to do something, just tell him it's impossible.'"

"While I learned a lot during that time, I managed to miss a few things about the real world. I feel so . . . different, so ignorant of life. . . . I never really had many friends. I fell behind other people my own age."

Laura rose and went to him, sliding her hand to the thick blond waves overlapping his starched white collar. "You're not behind anyone, Alex," she said warmly.

"Laura . . ." He shook his head in frustration. "Figure it out, Laura. Do I have to say it? I've been out of commission for most of the last five years. Don't you get it?"

It came to her even as he spun away from her, forcing out the words she should have guessed at long before.

"I've never been with a woman, Laura. I'm a virgin."

7

THEIR EYES LOCKED and Laura stood perfectly still. Her open palms were resting lightly on Alex's chest. Through the barrier of his smooth cotton shirt she felt the heat of his skin and the surge of his heart.

Words. Somewhere in the thick fog of her mind she knew there were the right words. She was so good at talking. Talking was her game. She should say something now to make it all okay. Alex needed her reassurance.

She moved her hand toward the exposed skin of his upper chest. Her fingertips paused at the side of his throat where his pulse thrummed angrily. Words were not what he needed.

And they weren't what she needed, either.

He stood absolutely still as she eased onto her tiptoes and brushed the soft, yielding heat of his lips. Just a touch; not a kiss, really. There had to be a way to express the tenderness she was feeling. It was so sweet—like the warmth that flooded her body now.

She caressed the rough edge of his jaw. It felt so foreign to her and yet so right. The supple give of his lips came as a surprise. Her hands trembled. How odd. That had never happened to her before.

"Laura." The word came out strangled. Alex still hadn't moved. His arms stayed stiffly by his sides, fists clenched.

The force of his need scared her but she didn't want
him to know that. All he had to know was how right this
was, how good it felt wanting him.

"Shh." The sound was a barely audible exhalation. As
she said it, her mouth found his lips again. This time she
trailed her tongue over them delicately and when she
pulled away, she saw them sheened by her touch.
Sheened like his eyes, which had become dark green
shimmering oceans—beckoning, seductive.

She stepped back. This was what he wanted, wasn't
it? Lord knew it was what she wanted. Didn't Alex know
that?

Yes. He read her mind. "Laura," he groaned, reaching
for her and sweeping her up into his arms effortlessly. He
strode to the bedroom and laid her on his bed, so easily,
so tenderly, she felt as weightless as she had that night in
the pool.

His water bed undulated beneath her. Standing over
her, Alex tore at his shirt.

"No," she murmured. "Let me."

He sat down next to her, waiting.

She moved to undo the first button. He watched her
hands with hypnotic fascination. A tantalizing sense of
power washed over her. *The feel of my fingers on his
button. That's all it takes.*

She watched her fingers now, as he did. The precise,
delicate slide of button through hole. The sudden release. The sharp intake of breath—his and hers. The
amazing discovery of flesh exposed by her own hand,
dark against the moon-bleached whiteness of his shirt.
The enticing trail of hair leading to yet another button.
Again the hard expanse of abdomen, clenched to steel-
iness.

One more and his shirt was free. She sat up and eased her hands onto bare, muscle-curved shoulders. He bit his lip and stifled a groan.

A touch—barely a touch—and he was lost to it. Seeing him, Laura felt it, too: the power he'd given her; the power he had over her. With one fluid motion she slipped the shirt from his shoulders. He tugged it off impatiently, flinging it across the room, and reached for her.

Alex pressed her down onto the bed. "Laura." He said it again and again, like an incantation—as though even her name had power over him. Quickly he climbed over her and knelt, trapping her hips between thick-muscled thighs. Slowly, slowly, he lowered himself toward her.

She fell into his eyes, lost in them until his mouth was on hers—not hard, not soft, but searching, learning. They found a rhythm at once, as tongue danced with tongue. Her hands twined in his hair, urging him on. It was the longest kiss of her life, and she had no intention of letting it end.

Alex pulled away—but only for a moment—to read her. Reassured by her smile, he renewed his exploration. Combing his fingers through her hair, he rained kisses on her cheeks, her eyelids, the lobes of her ears, returning every so often to her kiss-swollen lips. He moved with such confidence that Laura half wondered if he was really as inexperienced as he'd claimed.

Then Alex kissed her again, harder, with less concern for her need than for his own. Slowly he lowered himself onto her, his hips beginning to move with the same sweet, subtle rhythm as his mouth. His hand ventured onto one of her breasts, gliding tentatively over her blouse as if he were afraid he might hurt her.

"Yes," she murmured throatily, taking his hand and moving it in gentle circles. She gripped his index finger and pressed it to her hardened nipple. He smiled with pleasure. Oh, the power she had.

Reluctantly Alex pulled away onto his knees. "Beautiful," he said huskily. "God, Laura, you're so beautiful."

It was his turn to unbutton, and she watched with the same rapt fascination. His brow furrowed with concentration, he made his way down the row, frustrated by the endless delay. She watched his eyes widen as he pulled back her blouse to reveal her black lace bra.

Her breasts rose and fell as she struggled for air, and he studied her reverently. Then gently he lowered his head, trailing kisses like soft petals until Laura was afraid she'd faint from the sweet torture of it.

Alex eased a hand behind her back, and at first she thought he was trying to pull her closer. She could feel his fingers fumbling with the back of her bra. It took her a minute to realize he was trying to unfasten it.

"Here," she said softly, guiding his hand to the front closure.

He smiled nervously and went to work on the clasp. Only inches from her straining breasts, he muttered an expletive under his breath.

"Let me," Laura murmured, moving to assist. He wasn't the first male in history to fight this battle.

"No." He brushed her hand away, his voice tense. "I can do it."

He was embarrassed. She could feel that now. And yet it was such a silly thing. The kind of thing a boy would care about.

But Alex *was* a boy. He should be making out with girls in the back seat of a car at a drive-in. His first time should be a joyful adventure. Not a self-conscious performance where the only thing on his mind was the review he'd receive the next morning.

"Alex—" She moved to sit up and he rolled onto his side.

"I almost had it," he growled.

She stroked his cheek with the back of her hand. "Alex." Laura took in a tremulous breath. "I don't think this is a good idea."

He stared at her, stunned and wounded.

"You should be with...with someone your age. Someone special."

"You *are* special."

"But I'm not the right person...for this." She began buttoning her blouse self-consciously.

"You mean *I'm* not right." Alex stood abruptly. In the moonlight his chest was as smoothly sculpted as a sand dune—all ridges and curves. "You mean," he continued, "I'm too goddamned inexperienced to satisfy you. You mean, 'Come back, Alex, when you know what the hell you're doing. I'm a busy woman.'"

"No, Alex. No." Her voice quavered. "It was wonderful. It was...perfect." How could she have let it go this far? What could she have been thinking? She was so preoccupied with feeling good, she forgot that Alex might end up by feeling bad.

"Right," he spat out. "Perfect."

"I just suddenly realized that this was all wrong, that I'd let it get out of control."

"Damn it, Laura. Leave me some shred of dignity." He stalked toward the door. "Get dressed," he ordered. "I'll call you a cab."

Laura straightened her clothes and entered the living room. She found him sitting at the piano, playing the song he'd written for her.

"Alex?" She touched his shoulder and he shuddered visibly.

"Cab's on its way." He continued playing.

"Please," she begged, "don't think this has anything to do with you."

Nothing. Only music in reply.

She tried again. "There'll be someone else. Someone right."

"I'm a big boy, Laura," he said at last. "Forget it. *I* have."

The problem was, she knew she couldn't.

LAURA SPENT the next few days preoccupied by two things: attending to the Universal account and avoiding Alex. Universal was less trouble at this early phase than she'd expected. Gordy's people were docile, and Laura's careful work in assembling a crack team was paying off.

Unfortunately, part of that crack team was Alex, and she had no choice but to deal with him. For the most part that was accomplished through third parties and memos. Laura had arranged for Alex to deal with her assistant and Rhoda.

There had been one horrible meeting on Wednesday afternoon when the whole group, Alex included, had gathered for a planning session. Sitting at the head of the conference table, Laura had done her best to keep the momentum going.

But he was hard to ignore. He sat—slouched was more like it—at the far end of the table with his battered Nikes propped on its mahogany surface. His form-hugging jeans and faded green T-shirt made a strong fashion statement amid a sea of yellow suspenders and silk ties. While the rest of the group took copious notes and hung on Laura's every word, Alex occupied himself with the daunting task of completing the world's longest paper-clip chain. When she asked for input from the floor, he was kind enough to point out that the jelly doughnuts provided for the session were stale.

To her relief, as soon as the meeting adjourned, he'd disappeared. In the two days since then, she'd successfully avoided all contact with him, and now the weekend beckoned, promising a hiatus. The truth was, she'd half expected Alex to quit the job after she'd rejected his "advances." Well, perhaps that wasn't quite the way to describe what had happened, considering she'd done more than her share of advancing. But she'd been worried sick that she'd bruised his ego. She'd actually had visions of him doing something horrendous like jumping off the Brooklyn Bridge.

Instead he seemed—at least on the surface—like his old rebellious self. With one significant difference: As far as he was concerned, she didn't exist. And for both their sakes, it was probably just as well.

At least her weekend promised diversion in the form of her Saturday-night date with J. Parke Burnett— "The Bachelor from Hell," as Rhoda had begun referring to him. After Laura returned her call, Margo had made all the necessary arrangements, right down to wardrobe suggestions: "Parke likes a woman to dress like a woman. And he's very old-world about dating. So leave your gold card at home and let him pay for everything."

At any rate, tomorrow she would go shopping for a "womanly" dress. Whatever that meant. Ahead of her loomed forty-eight Alex-free hours, time enough to get the Great Hubby Hunt back on track.

MARTHA INC. was a Park Avenue institution. It wasn't a regular haunt of Laura's, but she figured it was a safe bet for a woman doing her damndest to "dress like a woman."

But after two hours of watching a gracious saleswoman sweep in and out of the showroom with designer labels draped over her arm, Laura was beginning to have doubts. Not that feminine frocks were in short supply—all the major labels could be found at Martha's. It just happened that every time Laura settled on the perfect dress for J. Parke Burnett, it looked perfectly dreadful on her.

After thanking the saleswoman, Laura left the shop in frustration. Without any particular goal in mind, she made her way to the Upper West Side, enjoying the mild spring day. The cafés along Columbus Avenue were overflowing with people and the energy of the neighborhood was a welcome contrast to the sophistication of Park Avenue. She felt much more at home here.

Laura headed over to Broadway. Seized by a sudden whim when she passed by Charivari, she went inside. She had always loved the store, with its high-fashion Italian and American designs. Their clothes were on the cutting edge of fashion—perhaps too daring and attention grabbing by her standards, these days. But after having stared at demure dinner dresses all morning, she couldn't resist trying on a few things just for the fun of it.

She fell in love with a skintight black number. She looked great in it—when she sucked in her tummy. If she could just figure out a way to hold her breath for eight-hour stints, she'd have it made. Critically eyeing herself in the dressing-room mirror, she wondered if she had the nerve to wear it publicly. Somewhere she'd read no woman's knees should be exposed after the age of thirty. And this little baby exposed her knees and a whole lot more.

Laura decided to get an unbiased opinion. She left the safe harbor of her dressing room and headed out onto the shop floor. A salesgirl with a crewcut descended on her. "Excellent!" she enthused.

"I don't know . . ." Laura hedged. It was hard to trust the "unbiased" opinion of someone working on commission.

"Cash or charge?"

"Oh, I'm not ready to make a commitment, if you know what I mean."

"Yeah. Do I ever. When you're ready to commit, my name is Tara, okay?"

"Oh, go for it, Laura. You're a knockout."

Laura spun around. Behind a pair of dark Ray-Bans, she saw her ex-boyfriend, Gerald, wearing a black beret and sporting a rather pathetic mustache. She hoped he'd just started cultivating it.

"Gerald." She walked toward him, her hand extended, and was herded into a wan embrace.

"Laura, you look fabulous! How long has it been? Two years?"

"More or less, but who's counting?" She made a show of glancing around the store.

"What are you looking for?" Gerald inquired.

"A white uniform, of course. Where there's Gerald, can a student nurse be far behind?"

He laughed—not the least bit unnerved.

"Ah, Laura. That tongue of yours is as sharp as ever. Not that I can blame you. I *was* rather a pain in the butt, wasn't I?"

"You always had a gift for understatement."

Gerald wrapped an arm around her shoulder. His smile was warmer and more relaxed than she'd ever seen during their eighteen-month relationship. "Laura, dear." He sighed. "You know, I'm really sorry for all the crap I put you through. We were so *mismatched*."

She laughed. "What did we ever see in each other?"

"God knows. But it wasn't a complete waste. You definitely sharpened my debating skills."

Laura smiled. He really had mellowed. "You seem different, Gerald. Almost likable."

"I'll let you in on my secret."

"Please don't tell me you've joined some kind of cult."

"It's love, Laura. I'm hopelessly, helplessly, head-over-heels in love."

"Gerald!" She shook her head in amazement. "Gerald in love? Who is she?"

"You mean *where*. Right over there. My Leslie."

He pointed toward a corner of the store where two people stood thumbing through a rack of leather pants. One was a young girl of eighteen or nineteen; the other, a man in his thirties.

No wonder she and Gerald had had so much trouble. *He was gay.*

"G-Gerald," she stuttered. "Why didn't you tell me about this? I would have understood—"

"No, no, no." He rolled his eyes. "The *other* one."

Laura couldn't resist. "Let me guess. She's a candy striper, right? Gerald, there are laws against this kind of thing. You could at least wait until she gets her braces off."

"Go ahead, laugh." His tone suggested he'd heard it all before. "But she makes me happy, Laura. With Leslie I see things differently, I . . ." He trailed off. "I like myself better when I'm with her. What can I say? That's *amore.*

It makes you believe all things are possible." He removed his sunglasses and she saw that his gray eyes were glistening with tears. "Happiness—even for me."

She gave him a gentle kiss on the cheek. "I'm really glad for you, Gerald."

"Trust me on this one, kid. Hold out for the real thing. Accept no substitutes." He turned to leave, then added: "And Laura?"

"Yeah?"

"Buy the dress."

It was the first time she'd ever taken his advice.

THE FOUR SEASONS was a short cab ride from Laura's East Side co-op, but it lasted long enough for her to have time to grow nervous.

When was the last time she'd gone out on a blind date? Had she ever?

Oh, yes. She'd been fifteen at the time, but twenty years did little to erase the trapped and desperate feeling she'd experienced seeing *Rodan the Conqueror* with "Booger" Fitzpatrick.

She didn't suppose J. Parke Burnett would be picking his nose and trying to hold hands at the same time, however. And the Four Seasons wasn't exactly the front row of a monster movie, either.

No. Margo had sworn up and down that he was the catch of the year. With a name like J. Parke Burnett, how big a drip could he be?

The cab arrived all too soon. The Four Seasons offered excellent Continental cuisine in beautiful surroundings that changed with each season and some of the less obnoxious service to be found in the city.

As soon as she entered, Laura found herself being eyed by the maître d'. He seemed to approve of her new dress.

The maître d' found the Burnett reservation but indicated that Mr. Burnett had not yet arrived. "Would *madame* care to wait or be seated?" he asked.

"I'll go ahead to the table. I imagine Mr. Burnett will show up soon. Or maybe he'll chicken out," she quipped.

"Pardon?"

"Oh, nothing." She shrugged. "Blind date. Maybe he'll chicken out."

"That, *madame*—" the maître d' bowed "—would be the great mistake of Mr. Burnett's life."

Laura smiled. The charm was practiced but it worked just the same. "That's very kind of you."

"Not at all, *madame*. Merely accurate. Would you care to follow me?" With a measured pace he led her to a lavishly set table in the Four Seasons's romantic Pool Room, named for the reflecting pool that dominated the dining area.

He pulled out her chair and offered a cocktail, which she refused. Better to meet this man stone-cold sober— though a drink might settle the butterflies in her stomach. Good grief! She was an accomplished thirty-five-year-old woman. Why did she feel like an awkward teenager?

She looked across the room and saw the maître d' making his way back toward her. Behind him walked a tall man in his early forties wearing a tailored dark suit. He had dark hair touched with gray at the temples. Laura was sure it was him—J. Parke Burnett.

The Dream Date.

"Ah, Laura." Burnett advanced, hand outstretched, calling her by her first name as though they'd known each other for years. How should she return his greeting? Did people call him J. Parke? J.? Parke?

"Mr. Burnett," she decided, rising to shake his hand. "Laura Daniels. Pleased to—"

"But don't get up, Laura," Burnett interrupted. "Gentlemen should rise for a lady, but—" She heard the pause in his voice and thought she saw him wince as he took in her dress. "There's no need for you to rise."

They took their seats. Burnett turned to the maître d' and said, "I'll have a bottle of the Corton-Charlemagne—'84, if you have it."

"Yes, sir," the maître d' replied. "But may I suggest the '82? Our sommelier feels that the '84 requires more aging."

"No, you may not," Burnett snapped. "I ordered the '84, and I'll have the '84."

"Yes, sir." The maître d' left—but not before rolling his eyes in condescension.

"Nervy bastard," Burnett commented. "You can't let those sorts take an inch, you understand."

"I don't suppose I'd notice the difference between one vintage and the next," Laura offered.

"Have you ever been married?" Burnett asked without waiting for an answer. "Well, I have. Twice. My first wife couldn't stand wine. You're not one of those, are you?"

"No. I enjoy wine."

"Thank God for that." Burnett favored her with a smile. "My second wife took my whole wine cellar in the divorce. Pure spite, you understand. Pure female spite."

Laura bit her tongue at the sexist remark.

"Nothing against women, you understand," Burnett added. "A woman who's a woman. That's what I'm looking for, you understand. That's what I told that Morgenroth creature, you understand. A woman who's a woman."

"I understand," Laura said, struggling to keep the sarcasm out of her voice. She was beginning to wonder what Margo's refund policy was.

Burnett continued as though she hadn't said a thing. "A smile, for example. Women today never smile. I like to see a woman smile. Not walk around looking like they'd climb over their mother to get a promotion, you understand."

"Yes," Laura replied patiently. "I understand."

"Ah, the wine," Burnett observed. Laura noted that it was the maître d' who had returned to serve the wine—not strictly his job. Obviously he wanted to eavesdrop a bit.

"Be careful not to disturb the sediment, my good man." Burnett pointed an imperious finger at the maître d'.

"There won't be sediment, sir. It's a young, white wine."

"You *see* what I mean?" Burnett said in exasperation.

"I remembered I have to call someone," Laura blurted out. Who? Whom could she claim to call? "My secretary. I forgot to tell her something. Will you excuse me?"

"While we're opening the wine?" Burnett seemed shocked.

"Very important. I'll just be a minute." Laura got up, catching a snicker on the face of the maître d'.

"Well, get them to bring you a phone. Surely the Four Seasons—"

"Yes, sir," the maître d' interrupted, "but our cordless phone is out of order."

Laura shot him a look of gratitude, heading away from the table before Burnett could think of something else to keep her.

She found the pay phone near the front entrance and, barely suppressing her desire to bolt, dialed Rhoda's home number.

She answered on the third ring.

"Rhoda. Listen," Laura exploded in relief. "I'm at the Four Seasons and I am trapped in the date from hell! I am suing Margo Morgenroth for every penny she has."

"Not having fun?" Rhoda inquired sweetly.

"You have got to get me out of this. I don't care how you do it—call up and tell them to give me a message my co-op is burning, I don't care—but get me out of this! Quick, before I have to stick a steak knife in this man's throat."

"Oh, murder's so messy, Laura." For a moment Rhoda was silent. "Okay, okay. Hang in there. I'll come up with something."

Laura hung up the phone, steadying herself with a few deep breaths. Thank God for Rhoda. She'd come through.

Laura headed reluctantly back to her table, oblivious to the heads that turned to watch her walk by. Burnett got up as she arrived, and sat down again when she did.

"Well, business taken care of?" Burnett inquired frostily.

"Yes. Sorry."

"Well, I went ahead and ordered for both of us. The steak tartare. The best in the city, you understand."

"Steak tartare?" Laura repeated dully. The raw beef dish had never been something she could stomach. "I don't like steak tartare."

"You'll learn to like it. I have it often, all over town, you understand."

"Yes, but—"

"A lot of people say the Twenty-One Club for tartare, but this is better." Burnett flashed her a smile. "I know we'll get along well, but you're going to have to learn to smile more."

Should I just get up and walk out? Laura wondered. *And should I pause first to tell this man what an obnoxious cretin he is?* No, no. In this city you could end up having to do business with all sorts of people. It wasn't a good idea to go around making enemies—unless it was absolutely necessary.

Fortunately, Burnett did not require any actual conversation from her. He seemed perfectly content to go on and on, all by himself, as though she weren't there.

Good old Rhoda would get her out of this gracefully. She'd better. But it had been ten minutes since she'd called her. Ten minutes during which J. Parke Burnett had said "you understand" about two thousand times.

If help didn't come soon, Laura was going to walk out. Forget about how it would look. Forget about what Burnett would tell half the eligible males in Manhattan. If this was what dating was like, she'd become a nun. She wasn't Catholic, but maybe she could convert.

She looked up as a movement caught her eye. There, standing directly behind Burnett, was her rescuer.

Alex was wearing shorts, an ill-fitting suit jacket, and a loosely knotted tie over a Baltimore Orioles T-shirt. The outfit was like nothing ever seen before at the Four Seasons. The maître d' must have loaned him the jacket and tie, thereby keeping to the letter—if not the spirit—of the dress code.

Slowly shaking his head from side to side, Alex looked at her.

Obviously Rhoda had called him. In spite of their problems, Alex had rushed to her rescue.

Thirteen years too young, painfully inexperienced and dressed at the moment like Calvin Klein's worst nightmare, he was still her knight in shining armor.

She smiled and sent Alex a look of thanks.

"See? Now that's what I like," Burnett said. "A woman who smiles, you understand."

"Laura!" Alex shouted, causing Burnett to jump. "Laura Jane Daniels!" Alex rushed to her side. "It's me! Cousin Billy Ray, from Mobile!"

"Cousin Billy Bob?" Laura repeated.

"Billy *Ray*," Alex corrected. "Billy *Bob*'s still in the state prison. That fella he hit, up and died."

"Oh, no." Laura looked downcast. "Well, cousin Billy Ray, this is my good friend J. Parke Burnett."

"Mark?" Alex asked.

"Parke," Burnett corrected through clenched teeth. "J. Parke."

"Park, huh? Well, hell, what's next?"

"Your steak tartare." The maître d' appeared, setting the red mounds of meat before them. Clearly, Laura realized, the maître d' was not about to let go of this entertaining table.

"Jeez, Louise!" Alex erupted. "That's raw meat!"

"Steak tartare," Burnett managed.

"Raw beef! Well, I'll be. I mean, raw snake, raw 'gator, sure." He leaned close to Burnett. "Had me some raw muskrat." He paused for effect. "It's the brains that are the best part. Don't look like much, but you spread 'em on toast and—"

Laura saw the color drain from Burnett's face. Alex grabbed a chair from an adjoining table, turned it around and straddled it. "We got so much to talk about, Laura."

"We're on something of a date, you understand," Burnett said.

"Well, don't mind us," Alex continued. "Laura and I can catch up on family. We'll just explain all the names to you. It'll be fun."

"I see." Burnett was groping for a graceful exit. "Oh, my goodness," he announced, feigning anxiety, "I entirely forgot about this report that's due—"

"Well then, Laura, you and I can go out and do the city up right." Alex laughed. "I hear they have all-night movie theatres over in Times Square."

Sixty seconds later, Alex and Laura burst out onto 52nd Street, laughing like schoolchildren who'd pulled a prank.

"Oh, boy, do I owe you, Alex!" Laura giggled, and tears ran down her cheeks.

"Naw, it was fun." He had dropped the tie and jacket with the grinning maître d' on their way out. "But you're going to have to loan me cab fare. I ran out with five bucks in my shorts."

"Gladly. But can I buy you dinner, at least?"

Alex smiled. "I don't expect a payoff for helping you out, Laura. Just lend me five to get home."

He was letting her off the hook so easily. But did she want to be let off? Now that he was here with her, she felt a sudden, strong desire not to let him go away—not to lose the moment.

But Alex had already hailed a cab that screeched up to the curb. The cabbie stared disbelievingly at them. Even by New York standards, they made an odd couple.

"You take this one," Alex said. "You shouldn't be out on the street in that dress. You're going to start a riot. But first—" he held out his hand and Laura fished in her purse for the money.

"Alex . . ." she began.

"Don't." He shook his head. "Nothing's changed."

Laura knew she should say something. She just wasn't sure what it was. "Thanks, Alex. You were great."

"Good night, Laura," he answered softly, holding the cab door open for her.

As the car pulled quickly away, she turned to see him looking after her, a dark silhouette in the light of a streetlamp. "You know something?" Laura said to the cabdriver. "I'm a fool."

"Whatever you say," the driver agreed cheerfully.

8

LAURA REACHED for the TV remote control on her night stand and clicked the "on" button. Huge shadows danced jerkily over the walls, as her darkened bedroom sprang to life with flickering light. On the screen of her portable television an old black-and-white movie was playing. She recognized it as "The Big Sleep." Alex Shaw had been responsible for many changes in her life—one of the most annoying was insomnia. If there was no chance of sleeping, Laura decided she might as well be productive.

She placed a cherry-red throw pillow on her lap and pulled a leather-bound notepad out of her nightstand drawer. Laura found the moments before she fell asleep particularly fertile for problem-solving. Frequently she was seized by a solution to some crisis at Tate and O'Neill and was able to get it down on paper just before she drifted off.

Tonight the problem was bigger than any she'd ever faced at Tate and O'Neill. She was determined to solve it, jot it down on her notepad for safekeeping, and get a good night's sleep.

The problem was Alex.

She reached for her pen and wrote "Goals" at the top of the page. There. That seemed like a logical place to start.

Her life had been the product of painstaking planning. Some might even have called it obsessive. But they weren't a hairbreadth away from being named partner at one of the country's most prestigious ad agencies. And they didn't drive Jaguars.

So what did Laura want?

She tapped her pen on her notepad, considering. Under the heading she wrote: 1. Career Fulfillment.

Nice fancy words, but what did she mean exactly?

Laura crossed them out and wrote: 1. Partner T and O'N.

That seemed too specific. Was that all she planned on doing with her next thirty-odd years of employment?

She tried again. This time: 2. Pie-in-the-Sky Alternative—Own Agency.

She liked the look of the words on paper but they scared her, too. With your own agency, there were so many variables. So many things that could go wrong. Things you couldn't plan for.

On to number three. 3. Financial Security. But if she had number one, number three was assured.

Next! She scribbled number four down before she lost her nerve: 4. Committed, Loving Relationship.

She was on a roll now. 5. Kids. She decided to leave the number unspecified.

What the heck. Number six could be a catchall category: 6. House, Dog, Picket Fence, Etc . . .

There. She perused the list—that wasn't so hard.

No, the hard part was figuring out how to obtain numbers four through six and possibly number two.

How had she obtained numbers one and three? Hard work, careful planning, and by knowing just what she wanted.

Not that she'd exactly wanted to go into advertising from the start. She'd been an English major planning on teaching high school. But she'd been working as a temp during grad school, and one of her first jobs was as a receptionist at a small ad agency out on Long Island. When their copywriter had decided to pursue more lucrative work as a used-car salesman, Laura had been pressed into service until the agency could find a replacement. But no replacement was necessary, since she fell in love with the ad business virtually overnight.

Okay. So she hadn't exactly planned that.

Her rise up the corporate ladder at Tate and O'Neill—now *that* had been planned. From junior copywriter to account executive to a junior vice presidency—every step had been calculated to propel her to the top.

Well, almost every step. There was that time when Bert Quincy contracted food poisoning at a sidewalk hot-dog stand. She'd only been at the firm a few months when she found herself supervising Bert's accounts. Soon she was given the title to go along with the work.

Laura let out a long, low sigh. There was something a tad unnerving about the notion that her whole career hinged on a used-car salesman and a bad chili dog.

Could it be that things weren't always as black-and-white as she'd assumed? That there was a murky arena where fate and free will overlapped?

What was it Alex had said to her? *Life is what happens to you while you're making other plans.* Certainly that was true in his life. Maybe it was true for her as well. While she had been making careful plans these past few weeks, plenty had happened.

Suddenly she remembered her encounter with Gerald. Love, he'd told her, makes you believe all things are possible.

Slowly she added one last item to her list: "7. Alex."

On the TV screen Lauren Bacall was making a seductive entrance in a big mink coat. Laura owned a three-quarter-length fake fur, herself. It wasn't mink, but it was close enough.

Could she pull it off? There was no way she'd have the nerve. Was there? Had she finally found a perfect occasion for fur?

IT WAS NEARLY two-thirty in the morning when Laura arrived at Alex's apartment. He answered the door wearing a tattered terry cloth robe and a dazed I-was-already-asleep expression. He leaned against the doorframe with his arms crossed over his chest.

"Hi," Laura said softly. "Isn't this the part where you invite me in?" she ventured, in her most sultry voice.

Alex eyed her with suspicion. "I suppose," he answered finally. "Come on in."

He stepped away from the door and she walked in, trying her best to look confident.

Alex closed the door. His gaze swept the length of her body, taking in the fur coat and black high heels with understated appreciation.

"Another big date?" he asked sarcastically.

"In a manner of speaking." She nervously cleared her throat.

"I figured you were pretty much tapped out for the evening." Alex sauntered over to the window and leaned against the sill.

Laura couldn't take her eyes off his strong, solid legs as he walked. Her pulse quickened. *Take it easy. You've got all the time in the world. This is a seduction and you want to get it right the first time.*

"I couldn't sleep," she told him.

"And?"

"And I figured you'd still be awake."

Alex looked unconvinced.

"Well, you're a musician, you keep crazy hours. It's still early for you." She sat down on his piano bench, crossing her legs demurely. "Aren't you going to offer me something to drink?"

Alex slapped his palm against his forehead in a parody of remorse. "Where are my manners?" He made his way toward the kitchen, studying her blatantly. "May I take your coat?"

"Oh God, no," she blurted out. "I mean, I think it's quite cool in here.

Alex shrugged. "Personally, I find it warm." He slouched in front of the refrigerator, investigating its contents. "Want a beer?"

"Yes, thank you. A beer would be lovely."

Alex opened two bottles and returned to the living room. "Here." He handed one to Laura unceremoniously. "No glasses."

"That's okay." She took a sip from the long-necked bottle.

"They're all dirty."

"Really, that's okay."

Alex leaned against the piano and took a long swig of beer. "So," he said tonelessly, "you couldn't sleep."

"No." Lord, she was bad at this. She didn't have a seductive bone in her body.

"You try counting sheep?"

"No, I never could get the hang of that. I start out fine, but soon they're jumping around my head in pairs and I lose count."

"Sounds a little Freudian to me."

Now *there* was an opening. "I *do* have these erotic daydreams sometimes," she confessed, her cheeks positively boiling.

"Don't we all." For all his enthusiasm, he might as well have been discussing dental plaque. She'd just have to ease into this gently. Alex was clearly in no mood to take a hint.

"Then I decided to use the time productively."

"Why doesn't that surprise me?"

She ignored the jab. Setting her beer on the floor, she inched closer. "I made a list."

"Another wish list for your friend Margo?" he asked harshly.

"A wish list for me." She took a deep breath. "I think I've finally figured out what I want in a man."

"Oh, not *this* again," Alex sneered. "Let me guess. He should be tall—"

"Yep." She nodded.

"Dark—"

"Blond, I think."

He blinked. "And handsome—"

"Oh, absolutely." Laura let her eyes stray to the tempting expanse of chest where his robe had opened.

"And rich, if I don't miss my guess."

"Who cares?" She held up a finger. "He should be creative, though. Rich in spirit."

Alex cocked his head to one side. "Creative, you say?"

"Mmm-hmm. Like a musician, for example." She gave him a wicked smile. "Someone with good hands." *Well, she was getting the hang of this, after all.*

"Good hands," Alex repeated slowly. He set his beer aside and studied his fingers with exaggerated care. "Yes—" He caught her gaze and held it. "Yes, I can see why good hands would be important."

"There's more."

"Of course there's more." He grinned tolerantly.

"He should adore anchovies."

Alex's smile faded. He stepped closer, shaking his head. "Laura, there's something you should know."

"You can tell me anything," she urged.

"I despise anchovies."

It was time. Laura stood and faced him, her heart glowing, her knees wobbly. "Alex?"

"Yes?"

"You can take my coat now."

He searched her face, looking for clues. In response she let the coat fall open. A light shrug and it began to slither off her shoulders—which were bare.

Like the rest of her.

All color drained from Alex's face. He stared, mesmerized, like the witness to a miracle.

The coat slipped to the floor.

Laura stood her ground, bathed in Alex's gaze. Her nipples stiffened as though he'd touched her. At last she saw what she'd wanted to see.

Alex *smiled*.

"Wanted to make damn sure there were no complicated buttons or snaps for me to get hung up on, eh?"

She smiled back. Alex understood. This was going to be fun, not some test.

"Now you see why I couldn't sleep."

He stepped closer. "I think maybe I could help you with that problem."

"I think so, too," she purred.

"I've got these great hands, see?" He held them up for inspection. "But they need a little training." His eyes glittered with raw energy.

Laura struggled to locate her voice. "I think that could be arranged."

Alex was within millimeters of touching her. Beneath his robe, his arousal was a poorly kept secret. Suddenly his smile evaporated. "I mean it, Laura," he said forcefully. "It has to be right. I want you to be happy."

"I will be." Her tone left no doubt. She moistened her lips with her tongue and consulted his face one more time.

Yes, he was ready.

Laura laced her fingers through his. "Time for night school." Wordlessly she led him to the bedroom and stationed him next to the water bed. Kicking off her shoes, she turned on the lamp next to his bed.

"Lesson number one," she began with a smile that put to rest any doubts about her talents at seduction. "Sometimes it's better with the lights *on*."

Alex returned her smile, intensifying it. "Should I take notes?"

Laura shook her head. "All my exams are open-book."

"Good," Alex replied. "'Cause I'd never cheat."

"I like that in a student." Laura reached for his belt, feeling wonderfully brazen. She tugged lightly—not enough to loosen it completely, but enough to make Alex shudder. "Lesson two," she continued, adopting a coyly instructive tone. "What's good for the goose—" she gave another tug, a little harder this time "—is good for you, too."

She pulled the belt free and eased Alex's robe off his shoulders. The sight of his perfect male form, resplendent in the soft yellow lamp-glow, played havoc with her lesson plan. God, the man was beautiful.

"Lesson number three?" Alex's voice was urgent.

Laura closed her eyes, fighting off the lush, lazy heat that threatened to drug her into speechlessness. "Lesson three," she managed at last, opening her eyes. "Female anatomy."

"I think I'm going to like this class."

"Wait till we get to male anatomy."

Alex's chest rose with a deep inhalation. "Maybe we should skip ahead. I'm an awfully quick study." He extended his right hand, preparing to touch her, but Laura intercepted it with her own.

"Lesson three," she whispered, bringing his hand to her lips and dusting soft kisses on the tips of his fingers. "Great hands, by the way."

He acknowledged her compliment with a terse nod.

"A woman's body," Laura continued, still holding his hand, "is like a piano."

"Then you're definitely a Steinway, baby," Alex said roguishly, scalding her with his gaze.

"Yes, well, in any case . . ." She'd completely lost her train of thought. "Oh, yes. A piano. The sound you produce from a piano depends on the subtlety of your touch."

"And you said you couldn't play," Alex teased.

"I can't." Laura smiled knowingly. "But you certainly can. Now, as I was saying, the response you get from the instrument depends on your touch. There's soft, for example." She led his hand to her breast and trailed his fingers delicately over the silken skin.

"Pianissimo, we call that," Alex offered in a ragged voice.

Laura shook off the heady rush of longing overtaking her. "Of course, you can vary the touch, to produce different effects." She cupped his hand over her breast, increasing the pressure incrementally as she moved his hand in languid circles.

On his own initiative, Alex captured the other breast in his free hand. A moan escaped her lips.

"That would be forte," Alex observed wryly. "Apply more pressure and you get a louder response."

"There . . . are . . . other techniques. . . ." She lost her voice, hypnotized by Alex's gentle ministrations.

"I'm listening," he encouraged.

"Other techniques like—What's that where you slide up and down the keyboard?"

"Glissando."

"Yeah, glissando." Reluctantly she removed his right hand and glided up and down her side.

Alex picked up the hint, pulling her closer as he ran his flattened palm up and down her back, pausing to cup her bottom. "I know one," he said, skating his fingertips along her spine.

"I'm listening." She barely managed the words.

"How about a chord, where you touch several keys at once? Say I start with this note—" he brushed his palm lightly over her sensitive nipple "—and then I add another one."

Before she could answer, he found her lips. He explored and brushed and lingered. His touch was so infinitely varied she could barely keep up. Dazed with need, she allowed herself to melt against his body, using him for support.

He eased his lips away and began to explore her neck with equal fervor.

"That," she whispered breathlessly, "would be a *major* chord."

He laughed appreciatively, pulling Laura toward the bed.

"When you said you were a quick study, you weren't kidding," Laura remarked, falling into his arms. They rolled onto the water bed and Alex pinned her down gently.

"I think perhaps I should apply what I've learned so far," he said, trailing kisses along her collarbone. "What do you think, teach?"

"I think yes." Laura wrapped her fingers in his hair and watched as he moved his mouth with slow-motion tenderness over one breast, then the other. Delightful ripples of sensation eddied deep inside her.

"Okay?" he lifted his head to ask softly.

"Very okay," she murmured. "Perfect."

While his tongue moved featherlike over her breasts, Alex's right hand embarked on a meandering tour of her abdomen. "It may be time for the next lesson," he suggested under his breath as the tips of his fingers neared their destination.

"You seem to be doing fine on your own." Somehow the line between teacher and student was rapidly becoming blurred.

He rested his hand lightly on the spot most in need of attention. His stillness was an exquisite tease.

"Hmm." His eyes shone with the lustre of desire. "Well, it seems to me the same basic principles should apply." Tenderly he explored with the tip of his finger, watching for her response.

"Oh," she groaned.

"There?"

Laura nodded mutely.

"And there?"

"Mmm."

"I'll take that as a yes." He moved deeper, more confidently, and Laura reached instinctively for his arm.

"What?" Alex stopped instantly. "Did I hurt you?"

"Oh, no," Laura gasped. "Far from it. I just didn't want you to stop." She eased up on her elbows and kissed him lightly. *"Ever."*

Alex smiled in relief. "Listen," he ventured thickly, "I was thinking about maybe going for some extra credit."

She watched as he made his way down the length of her body with agonizing slowness, settling at last between her thighs.

Then she couldn't watch any longer, closing her eyes to the delicious things he was doing to her body. Things no man had ever been able to do to her body. Rapturous, dazzling things—

"Laura?"

From somewhere, far off, came Alex's voice. She opened her eyes slowly.

"Am I doing okay?"

She answered with a blissful, awestruck smile.

"Is there anything else I can . . . do?" Alex asked.

Laura reached for him and pulled him toward her. "If you do any more," she said, "I'm going to pass out."

His reaction to her words gave Laura as much pleasure as his touch. In one fluid movement she slipped from underneath him and rolled to one side. Easing him onto his back, she climbed on top. His eyes feasted on her with absolute reverence. "Have you forgotten lesson four?" she chided. "Male anatomy?"

"I'd rather work on lesson three some more." Alex cupped her breasts in his hands. "I know my own body."

"Not as well as I'm going to, by the time we're done." She kissed him then, a lusty, no-nonsense kiss, and Alex shuddered beneath her. She moved away and let her mouth linger over the breathtaking shoulders she'd admired for so long. "Great shoulders," she commented throatily.

"Keep talking, Laura," Alex urged. "I love hearing your voice."

She moved to a nipple and stroked it with her tongue. Looking up, she found Alex biting his lower lip, stifling a low groan. "Great nipples, too," she teased.

Her tongue ran a trail through his chest hair. "Great chest," she murmured. She followed the dusting of hair down his abdomen with her lips. He clenched at her touch, and it was Laura's turn to moan. "God, how I've wanted you." Laura heard her own voice and marveled at it. She'd never liked to talk during sex, preferring quiet so she could concentrate. Now each word she spoke seemed provocative and very, very sexy.

"You know," Laura remarked as her fingers raked the bristly hair of his thighs, "I just don't feel I'm as well acquainted with your body as I'd like to be." She smiled coyly. "Maybe what I need is an extra-credit assignment."

From the guttural growl that escaped his lips when she touched her lips to him, Laura knew he agreed.

Sweet minutes passed before Alex pulled her to him. "I've got to have you, Laura," he whispered urgently. "Now." The wild light in his eyes silenced her. She placed his hands on her hips and saw his eyes darken fractionally.

"What is it, darling?" she asked.

"Is it . . . I mean, are you okay?"

Her eyes closed, then brightened. "Oh, you mean birth control?" She laughed. "Don't worry. My trusty diaphragm's already on duty."

"Pretty cocky, weren't you?"

"The same could be said of you, my friend."

She met him now gently, easing down with greedy delay. Lowering her body onto his, she pressed her breasts against his chest.

They kissed, and suddenly Alex rolled, holding her close, so that Laura was beneath him. "Tell me," he demanded. "Tell me what you want, Laura."

She wrapped her legs around him. "This," she managed at last. "Slow, like this."

Alex moved with tortured slowness, forcing restraint, clinging to what little self-control remained. Laura dug her fingers into his back, moaning. He stopped moving then, stopped breathing, even. "Shh," he rasped. "Don't move. Give me a minute."

Laura. He thought only of Laura, willing himself to hang on. She **was** everything. She was all that mattered.

Again he began the slow, even stroking that seemed to give her so much pleasure.

"Alex," she whispered, "I'm so close." Her eyes were shut, her breath coming in little rasps.

He kissed her softly.

"It's so perfect," she said, opening her eyes to reveal a shimmer of tears.

"Of course," he told her with gentle confidence. "It's love."

She cried out then, and he lost himself in her, letting go at last to something beyond them both.

It had all been so easy. If only he'd known.

"Laura?" He kissed her again, wiping away her tears.

"Yes, love?"

He smiled transfixed, unable to find any words. At last he knew what to say.

"Wanna do it again?"

IT WAS NEARLY DAWN by the time they fell asleep in each other's arms, drained, exhausted.

Alex woke first, careful not to disturb Laura. He fumbled around for the clock and, finding it, pulled it toward him.

Ten forty-eight. Well, normally that would be pretty close to his usual rising time. But today it meant he'd gotten slightly less than six hours' sleep. Still, he didn't feel tired.

A grin broke out on his face. No, he didn't feel tired at all. He had just spent the greatest night of his life.

He reveled in his memories of last night—the point at which Laura had... And when she did.... Life *was* good. His life had taken a turn for the good as unexpectedly as it had taken a turn for the worse, five years earlier.

If there had been no accident, no pain, no confinement, there might not have been a Laura. If you're happy today, Alex, then you can't regret any part of what brought you to this point. And if Laura would be his—not for a night, but forever—then he'd gotten a damn good deal.

Laura shifted in her sleep and lay on her back now, breathing lightly. The sheet barely covered her slowly rising and falling breasts. He gently pulled the sheet down.

Yes. She was as beautiful as he remembered.

He wondered if she was ready to get up. And if so, surely there were *better* ways to wake up than to the alarm clock's electronic beep.

Much better ways.

LAURA HAD NEVER quite felt this way waking up. Lingering on the edge between sleeping and waking, she rolled to one side, her back pressed against Alex. She felt his hands rhythmically stroke her breasts, her thighs.

She savored his touch as she slowly awakened and then turned to face him, smiling dreamily.

Suddenly she sat bolt upright. "I'm late for work!"

"Laura, Laura." Alex laughed. "It's Sunday, woman."

"Ohh." She sank back into her pillow.

"I don't suppose you'd want some coffee if, if I were to make some?"

"I'll help. I'm awake." She climbed out of the bed, teetering sleepily. "Or I soon will be."

"I'll make coffee. You can have the shower first. I'd join you, but it's a small shower."

"Wanna go have brunch someplace?" she inquired, yawning hugely.

"Sure." Alex chuckled. "I'll wear jeans and a shirt. You wear what you had on last night."

"Oh, jeez. I forgot about that." She giggled guiltily. "I guess that wouldn't look too suspicious, a woman out on a warm Sunday morning in a fur coat. Period."

"Totally inappropriate," Alex agreed. "Shouldn't be seen in fur before eight in the evening, in my opinion as a fashion maven."

"So I'm stuck here all day?" Laura said in mock horror.

Alex took a deep breath. "Well, we'll just have to make the best of it."

9

"I NEVER THOUGHT I'd see the day." Rhoda entered Laura's office with a look of awe on her face.

"So I'm going home at five o'clock. So what?" Laura said, smiling slyly.

"For the second week in a row? Keep up this goof-off attitude, young lady, and I'm going to put in for your job."

"Think anyone else has noticed?" Laura asked lightly, piling memos into a foot-high stack.

"Noticed? You're the talk of the break room." Rhoda leaned heavily against Laura's desk. "Well, right after Carol Merriman's affair with the water-cooler guy."

"At least I'm in good company."

"There are many theories, of course. You're jumping ship to another firm, you're burned-out, you've got terminal spring fever. Only I know the real reason, and I've been sworn to secrecy."

"You know, Rhoda, I could really get used to this love stuff." Laura grinned.

"I've never seen you so happy. It's obnoxious."

"I've never *been* so happy."

"Me either, actually," Rhoda remarked. "Ever since you and Alex became an item, my work load's dropped by half."

Laura shook her head. "The amazing thing is, I'm still here, Tate and O'Neill's still here, and the world has managed to go on spinning. Guess I'm not quite as in-dispensable as I thought."

"Surprise, surprise." Rhoda favored Laura with her patented maternal look. "So, when are you guys going to make this thing public?"

"I don't think we're exactly required to take out an ad in the *Times*. Lots of people know, anyway. You, Larry, a few people who matter. It's just that neither of us wants to make a big deal out of an office romance. You know how people are."

Actually, the low profile was more her idea than Alex's. He would have preferred renting space on the side of the Goodyear blimp. But there was no point in getting Rhoda started.

"How about your mom?" Rhoda asked a little skeptically. "Does she know?"

"I mentioned it to her on the phone last weekend. I told her that Alex and I were . . . seeing each other socially," Laura hedged.

"And what did she have to say?"

"Well, I think she was disappointed that Alex wasn't more interested in Celeste. She had them paired up. And," Laura added, "I'm not sure Mom entirely grasps what the relationship is between Alex and me."

"You're breaking it to her slowly, eh?" Rhoda shook her head disapprovingly. "I don't think you're giving her enough credit. I honestly believe if you give people the chance, they'll get over the age thing."

Maybe Rhoda was right, Laura reflected—at least as far as her mother was concerned. But she herself had a long way to go to get over "the age thing." She still had too many moments of self-consciousness when she was out in public with Alex. It was probably just her imagi-nation, but it felt as if people stared at them a second or

two longer than was strictly polite. Young girls would eye
Alex with keen interest until they glanced at her. Then
you could just watch the wheels turning as they considered the possibilities—"I hope he's not your son, and I
know he can't be your boyfriend. So he's got to be your
younger brother, right?"

Naturally Alex was oblivious to all this. Even oblivious to the looks from other men that dismissed him as a
gigolo. Alex was proud of her. Proud to be seen with her
all over Manhattan. Which in theory was flattering and
sweet. Unfortunately, Laura was rapidly developing a
severe case of street paranoia, over and above the standard New Yorker vigilance.

"Since we're on the subject of age, let me try just one
last time." Rhoda interrupted her reverie. "I'm absolutely, positively, not allowed to mention your birthday
this Friday?"

Laura rolled her eyes. "How many times do I have to
explain this? Thirty-five is just a number. It means nothing in and of itself."

"Don't go all existential on me," Rhoda protested. "I
just asked."

"Age is just a state of mind. People's ages are not important." Laura winced. Even to her own ears she
sounded defensive.

"Well, if it's irrelevant, why do you care if I get you a
birthday card?" Rhoda countered reasonably.

"Because it *is* irrelevant. I intend to ignore it and," she
added, "all subsequent birthdays."

"What are you going to do that night, then?" Rhoda
asked suspiciously. "Sit home alone and gorge on ice
cream?"

Laura patted her on the shoulder. "I guess we'll just have to hope for the best. Besides, Alex will probably hang around to keep me company."

A slow smile dawned on Rhoda's face. "Well, that's birthday present enough for any woman. But I'm still going to get you a card." Suddenly she gasped. "Whoa! What a punt!"

"The baby?" Laura laughed.

"This kid has National Football League written all over him."

"What if he's a girl?"

Rhoda shrugged. "There's always girls' rugby."

As they moved to leave, Laura clicked off her desk lamp. She glanced around her office, which was bathed in late-afternoon sun, and wondered for a moment how this room could ever have seemed like the center of the universe. There were other things—far more important things. Like Rhoda's baby kicking, or joking with her mom on the phone. Or knowing that Alex was waiting for her at home with a song, a shoulder rub and much, much more.

No wonder she went around all day with a smile on her face. She couldn't help it.

As SHE INSERTED the key in her door, Laura caught Alex's muffled voice and the smell of freshly brewed espresso. In very short order, she'd gotten used to the idea of coming home to him. It hadn't been nearly the shock to her hyperorganized world she'd expected it would be.

They'd exchanged keys for the sake of convenience more than anything else. It had been Alex's idea, but he didn't regard their key exchange with the great significance she did. To Laura, having a key made for Alex, and getting one of his, was symbolic. Not exactly on a par with exchanging wedding bands, but not to be taken lightly either; it meant commitment. To Alex, it was simply practical.

Still, she liked the idea of letting down her barriers a bit. She'd been surprised at how comfortable the new arrangement was. Her privacy had always been very important to her and fortunately, Alex felt the same way. They slept together every night—well, sleep was hardly a top priority these days. But during the days, they went their separate ways. Alex's work for the firm was done mostly at his apartment and he showed up at the office only intermittently, breezing in on a schedule all his own. Even then, they rarely saw much of each other. And most nights he was at Mickey-O's, jamming until the wee hours.

So, as it turned out, Alex had been right on the money when he had tried to soothe her fears about, as she so delicately put it, "invading her space."

"You sound like you're inviting the Huns over for afternoon tea," he'd chided. "I have my own life to lead, Laura. We'll be lucky if we see each other at all. I understand that you're stuck in your ways—"

"I beg your pardon?" she'd demanded.

"But fortunately," Alex had continued, undaunted, "I'm flexible enough for both of us. Up to a point, that is. If you think I'm dragging out of bed to see your butt off to work at five in the morning, you've got another thing coming."

So, each morning she'd tiptoed softly out the door while Alex slept—hardly a major sacrifice. In fact, she'd made so few compromises, she almost wished for more. She wouldn't mind at all seeing Alex more than she did.

Laura entered the co-op to find Alex standing in the kitchen and talking on the telephone. He spun to greet her, looking taken aback. "Well, okay then," he mumbled into the phone. "I'll be sure she gets the message."

"Hi, gorgeous," Laura said, rushing to give him a long, thorough kiss. "Who was that?"

"That? Uh, that was Rhoda. Just Rhoda."

"Rhoda? What did she want?"

He looped his arm around her waist and pulled her close. "God, you smell good."

"I ought to, for two hundred bucks an ounce." She unbuttoned the top button of his shirt.

"Hey, what's the idea?" Alex protested teasingly. "Is that all I am to you? A sexual plaything?"

"No, but I'd say it's in the top ten." She trailed her finger over his breastbone. "So, what was it Rhoda wanted? I just saw her not half an hour ago."

"She wanted to remind you about your natural childbirth class."

"What about it?"

"Well, it's on as scheduled." He seemed suddenly fascinated by her neck. With great care, he began kissing a tender spot where her pulse had launched into some very interesting rhythms.

"Of course it is," Laura responded distractedly. "Why wouldn't it be?"

"Search me. You know Rhoda. She's very thorough." He moved toward the nape of her neck. "By the way, so am I. I'm doing a careful survey of your entire body—in case you hadn't noticed."

"Using your mouth?"

"Hands, too." He nodded seriously. "Hey, guess who else called today? Margo Morgenroth herself. Just picked up the phone and dialed like a regular person."

"What did *she* want?" Laura had written Margo a brief note after the debacle with J. Parke Burnett, explaining that her services would no longer be required.

"It seems she has another J. Parke clone on-line for you. Something about anchovies?"

Laura slipped a finger inside the waist of Alex's jeans. "Did you explain that I'm no longer in the market?"

"Yep." Alex's green eyes glittered as if they'd been dusted with gold. "Asked her what you'd want with some worn-out old guy when you could have a young stud like me."

"Alex!"

"She wanted to know if I had any brothers."

Laura dissolved into giggles. "Come on, young stud." She pulled him toward the bedroom. "Let's see if you live up to your billing."

Alex glanced at his watch. "I've got to be at the club in an hour. Still, I guess a warm-up never hurt." He raced her to the bedroom and they fell together onto the bed. "We're trying out a couple of new songs tonight and I'd really like it if you could stop by. Are you planning on coming?"

"Oh, Alex—" she smiled wantonly "—I have every intention of it."

ON FRIDAY AFTERNOON, Alex intercepted Laura just as she was stepping out onto Sixth Avenue from the Tate and O'Neill building.

"Hey, birthday girl," he called, hugging her from behind.

"Alex," she warned, "you *promised.*"

"A momentary lapse." He held up his hands in a show of innocence, falling in with her quick pace down the street.

"Like breakfast in bed this morning?"

He shrugged. "You know what a morning person I am. Can't get enough of that *Today* show."

"You were up at five," she said accusingly.

"Well you can safely rest assured *that* will never happen again. Oh— I forgot this." He passed Laura the funnel of green tissue paper he held in his left hand, and was delighted to see her grimace melt into the smile he loved.

"A white rose." Laura held the flower close, inhaling deeply. "Oh, Alex, it's beautiful."

"The flower lady said it was symbolic of something but she couldn't remember what."

"Purity of devotion, perhaps," Laura offered, squeezing his hand.

"I told her as long as it wasn't chastity, we were okay. Say, where are you going, anyway?"

"The dry cleaners. Then home. Don't forget you promised me we'd have Chinese delivered."

Alex nodded. "Kung Pao chicken from Fu's. I'm a man of my word."

Technically, anyway. Laura'd get her Kung Pao chicken, all right. She'd also be getting a couple of dozen uninvited birthday guests.

Alex draped his arm around her shoulder and gave Laura a nonchalant wink. He hoped he wasn't making a big mistake with this birthday bash. Rhoda and Celeste had thought it was a great idea, but he was the one who'd been warned repeatedly by Laura to keep the celebrating to a minimum.

All week he'd been making secret arrangements. He was beginning to feel more like a CIA agent than a lover. There'd been a clandestine rendezvous with Rhoda and Celeste, secret telephone calls and shopping expeditions. And he was starting to have guilt pangs about the whole exercise—less because of the secrets he was keeping from Laura than because of his fear that she'd be annoyed.

But he knew this birthday had to be special. And he wanted to show her in some tangible way how much he cared. The diamond pendant he'd found at Cartier had put a serious hole in his bank account, but hell—what did he care? Money had never mattered to him. When he had it, he spent it; when he didn't, he ate macaroni and cheese. He knew Laura had plenty of jewelry, but that didn't matter either. He'd wanted to get her something special and he felt pretty sure he had.

"Alex?" Laura asked as they turned the corner. "Did you see the way that girl was looking at you?"

"Give me a break. This is New York. There's at least a fifty-percent chance she was ogling you." He gave her a playful pat on the behind. "And who could blame her? Have I mentioned that you look absolutely gorgeous today?"

As they stepped into the tiny dry cleaners, he noticed that wistful look that signaled another attack of what Alex liked to think of as Laura's "bimbo fixation."

"You know," he said while she gave the old man behind the counter her receipt, "it's getting so we can't walk down the street without you freaking out over some bimbo in a cheerleader's outfit."

Nicely put, Alex. It is the woman's birthday, after all.

"I hardly 'freaked out,'" Laura replied as she accepted her blouses and handed the clerk a twenty. "I merely observed."

"I have my doubts about your powers of observation, my dear." He tenderly brushed back a wisp of hair from her forehead. "Can't you just relax a little and enjoy?" He knew he was pushing, but he desperately wanted her to feel as good about their relationship as he did.

"I am enjoying. I'm just not relaxing," Laura said with a self-deprecating smile.

"Do all women make things so damn complicated?"

"Yep," the salesclerk interjected. "Take my word for it, son."

"But *why?*"

The clerk leaned forward to whisper in Alex's ear. "They like to see us suffer," he said with absolute conviction.

"Wrong." Laura picked up her change from the counter. "We just like to keep you on your toes."

As they turned to leave, the old man added under his breath: "Nice work, son. My hat's off to you."

Alex chuckled as Laura whisked out the door.

"There!" she fumed when he caught up with her. "That's just the kind of thing I'm afraid of."

"What do you mean? He was just a harmless old guy."

"Didn't you find him . . . patronizing?"

"I dunno." Alex took the dry cleaning from her. Things were not going precisely according to plan thus far. "A little sexist, maybe. But he's from a different generation."

"Oh, *please.*"

Alex could tell Laura had shifted into her I'm-about-to-give-you-the-benefit-of-my-many-years-of-wisdom mode. He loved to hassle her when she really got pedantic.

"What that—sleaze bag—was saying was, 'Congratulations, kid. You must be keeping the old lady happy, but what's in it for you?'"

"So, aren't I?" He smiled, but she wasn't buying it.

"Aren't you what?"

"Keeping you happy?"

"I know this game, Alex." She held up a warning finger, fighting back the smile stirring on her lips. "You're being deliberately obtuse to piss me off."

"Is it working?" He could tell he had her now.

She paused. "Yes. Yes, I am now definitely pissed off."

"Good." He stopped in the middle of the sidewalk and pulled her close, crushing the dry cleaning between their bodies. He kissed her hard, silently praying he could trust to the natural indifference of New Yorkers.

"See?" he whispered. "No one even noticed."

"Wrong," Laura whispered back. "I noticed."

THEY ARRIVED AT Laura's co-op over an hour later. Alex had insisted on stopping by Mickey-O's for a piece of sheet music he'd left behind, and before long they were sitting at the bar listening to an old-time jazz musician spin stories about the greats he'd known and loved.

In spite of her best efforts, Laura was in a lousy mood by the time they got home. She'd really psyched herself into believing this birthday wouldn't bother her. After all, her mother had made a valid point when she'd joked, "Wait till you hit forty or fifty. Now, *those* are biggies."

But Laura still felt jittery. She just wanted to cuddle up with Alex in front of the TV and munch on fortune cookies—assuming they were filled with happy predictions. Oddly enough, Alex hadn't seemed nearly as rushed to get home as she was. It had practically taken a crowbar to get him out of Mickey-O's.

As she inserted her key in the lock, she had an awful premonition of what was going to happen next.

"*Surprise!*"

It was her worst nightmare—a *birthday* party.

She stood frozen to the floor, her jaw open to somewhere around navel level. A standing-room-only crowd
filled the living room; the kitchen picked up the over-
flow. They surged toward her like an angry mob.

The co-op was decorated in a funereal sort of way.
Black crepe-paper streamers hung from the ceiling. And
everywhere she looked there were black balloons with
Over The Hill printed on them. Even the cake on the
coffee table had black frosting. The couch was piled high
with gifts.

"Surprised?" Alex whispered from behind.

"Alex, you shouldn't have," Laura answered through
clenched teeth.

"She's surprised," Rhoda confirmed as she stepped
forward out of the mob to give Laura a hug.

"I mean, you *really* shouldn't have," Laura repeated
woodenly.

Rhoda winked at Alex. "She'll get over it. Give her five
years or so."

"Yeah," Celeste called as she fought her way through
the crowd. "If you behave yourself, we'll do it all over
again for the big four-O."

"I'll be sure to leave town that week." Laura glanced
around the room at the sea of faces. Larry and Ginger
were there, along with just about everyone she worked
with; her mom and dad, her Aunt Jenny, some cousins
she hadn't seen since her college days; and an assort-
ment of neighbors and casual friends. There were some
of Alex's friends from Mickey-O's she recognized, including Danny and Becky.

Beside her Alex waited expectantly. Laura took a deep
breath. No matter what, she couldn't bear to disappoint
him. He'd worked so hard. She had no right to be a jerk

about this. She might even end up having a good time—
stranger things had happened.

First things first. If Alex had been a relatively well-kept
secret, that was certainly the case no longer. She might
as well go for broke. *It's my party and I'll kiss if I want
to*, she sang to herself. She turned to Alex and give him
a very-hard-to-ignore kiss as the room broke into applause. Alex looked like he'd just won the World Series
of kisses.

For the next two hours Laura played the room for all
it was worth. She hugged cousins, kissed friends and
made small talk. After a glass of champagne, she began
to relax and even enjoy herself.

Once the gift-opening ceremony was over, she cornered Alex in the kitchen. "I hate to say you told me
so—" she ventured.

"That's okay." He kissed her lightly on the cheek. "I
love it."

"But you *did* tell me so." Laura studied the ceiling. "I
was so busy turning this birthday into a crisis, I forgot it
could just be fun. Well, thank you. I'm sorry I was so
uptight. Come on, let's go back in."

Before long, Alex and a few of his musician friends had
set up in the corner and begun playing. The guests di-
vided into two groups. Alex's friends, Rhoda, Celeste,
Ginger and Laura's assistant Mike D'Angelo—the un-
der-thirty crowd—composed one group. Everybody
else—Laura included—was in the other.

As she drifted back and forth between the two, Laura
began to feel increasingly schizo. The group assembled
around Alex was discussing a new MTV video when she
dropped by.

The more "geriatric" crowd was engaged in a heated
debate over the relative merits of tax-free bonds and

mutual funds. Neither discussion was particularly gripping.

Feeling strangely out of place, Laura gravitated back toward the kitchen. This was her home. These were her friends and family. And this was her birthday.

Barry Silverman sauntered in to refill his champagne glass. "Happy Birthday, kiddo," he said, slapping her on the back.

She could tell from the slurring of his words that he was not in need of a refill. "How are you getting home, Barry?"

"M' wife. You know, I'd give you a birfday kiss, Laura baby, but it looks like to me like you're getting plenty of that young stuff."

Laura clenched her fists, resisting the strong temptation to clobber him with the nearby champagne bottle.

"You know, there's a word for guys like Alex. Good ol' Alex," he continued, leering at her. "Gi-...uh, gig-.... Something like that."

"There's a word for guys like you, too, Barry," Laura said icily. "Ass-...uh, ass—Well, you get the idea."

"Gigolo, thas' it...."

She stormed out of the kitchen, shaking with anger. Around the corner she bumped into Rhoda.

"Hey, what's wrong, birthday girl? If it's that scarf I got you, I saved the receipt."

"I loved the scarf." Laura steadied her voice. "It's Barry I'd like to return to whatever slimy hole he crawled out of."

She slumped against the wall. "He made a crack about Alex and me."

Rhoda's expression darkened. "What a jerk. You're not going to let Barry's big mouth ruin your day, are you? Alex went to a lot of trouble to get things just right. Why, he must have called me a hundred times in the last two weeks trying to get everything organized. He was really worried you'd be mad that he made such a big deal over your birthday." She touched Laura on the shoulder. "Don't let it get to you, okay? Do you really care if Barry Silverman approves of your life-style? What's he got that's better?"

Laura forced a smile for Rhoda's benefit. "Well, when you put it that way. . ." She looked up to see that several guests were gathering up their coats. "Looks like the party's starting to wind down. Guess I should put in an appearance at the door."

"Laura?"

"Yeah?"

"Want me to go beat up Barry for you?"

Laura glanced at her friend's pregnant form. "Thanks champ. I'll take a rain check."

After another twenty minutes, most of the guests had departed. Laura was hanging in until the time arrived for the goodbye hug with her parents.

"That kid's got great hands," her father told Laura as they made their way toward the door.

Laura craned her neck and caught a glimpse of Alex in the midst of a boogie-woogie tune, pounding the keyboard of her grandmother's old upright piano.

"Yes, he does," Laura replied.

"Maybe we can all head down to the Village some night to hear him play," her father added.

Laura's mother embraced her in a warm hug. "Happy birthday, honey." She zeroed in on Laura's ear before whispering, "I hope you know what you're doing."

"Me too, Mom," Laura whispered back.

They were halfway out the door when Laura's mother turned back. "Just tell me this, dear. Are there sparks?"

"Mom," Laura answered without hesitation, "there are *fireworks*."

Mrs. Daniels gave a satisfied nod. "That's a good start."

Laura closed the door behind her parents, murmuring under her breath, "But is that enough?"

She wandered over to the piano where the band had just wrapped up its final number. "Know what?" she said to Alex, joining him on the piano bench. "I think you're pretty terrific."

"Feeling's mutual." He combed his fingers through her hair.

"Mind If I go crash in the bedroom? I could use a nap."

"Worn-out?"

She ran a finger over the piano distractedly. "Well, you know what a party animal I am."

"I'll get rid of these folks as quick as I can," Alex reassured her. "Then I promise: Kung Pao chicken and lots of fortune cookies."

Laura kissed him on the cheek and headed discreetly for her bedroom. Just what would her fortune be? she wondered absently. Where was all this going with Alex?

She collapsed on her satin comforter and tried to stem her unease. There were all kinds of reminders of the problems she and Alex faced as a couple, pricking away at her happiness. She couldn't even walk into the dry cleaners—for goodness' sake—without being made uncomfortable.

But the discomfort wasn't really about what other people thought of her. She hadn't gotten this far by trying to please the Barry Silvermans of the world.

The discomfort came from her own doubts about Alex. When it came to falling in love with Alex, she'd had no choice. But on the question of whether or not to stay with him, she did.

"Madam, your gourmet Chinese feast is being prepared even as we speak." Alex entered the bedroom and plopped down next to her. "Fu's said about twenty minutes."

Laura nestled her head on his shoulder. "Alex. Thank you for everything. It was wonderful." She kissed his chin. "*You* were wonderful."

"I know you had in mind something a little quieter, but I figured it'd be good for you."

"So you think you know better than I do what's good for me?" she asked lightly.

"Yes. Sometimes I do," he said seriously. "For example, remember when I first saw your office in all its arctic splendor? I told you you had primary colors written all over you." He pointed to the pile of vibrantly colored throw pillows at the foot of the bed. "I rest my case."

"Lucky guess."

"Nope. Men's intuition."

"It bothers me that anyone could know me better than I know myself. Especially when about half the time I don't seem to know me at all." She grimaced. "If you know what I mean."

"Amazingly, I do."

She pounded the bed with her fist. "It figures."

"Well, don't get me wrong. I'm not infallible. I never dreamed you were going to pull that mink-coat trick."

He grinned and the look of happiness on his face made her want to cry. Why was it that only *she* saw problems ahead for them?

"Oh, Alex," she blurted out, tears pooling in her eyes. "How come you're always so . . . so damn *happy* all the time? Why is all this so easy for you when it's so hard for me?"

"'This'?"

"You and me." Laura covered her eyes with her arm.

Alex lifted her arm and peeked. "This wouldn't be PMS in action, would it?"

"Is everything a joke with you?" she cried.

"Yes, pretty much. You'll find life can look bleak if you don't develop a sense of humor." He rolled off the bed and stood, hands on his hips. His smile had disappeared. "Why don't you cut to the chase, Laura? I've been walking around on eggshells ever since I met you and frankly, it's getting exhausting."

She fought back a heaving sob. "I just don't see us working out, that's all."

"And what the hell does 'working out' mean?" Alex demanded. Angry, he looked much older. "I thought we were 'working out' just fine."

She forced herself to say the words: "But what about a house or a dog or even a kid? We're on separate time lines and they're never going to intersect." Her lips trembled uncontrollably. "I just can't stop having these doubts."

"Doubts?" Alex shot back. "You wanna hear about some doubts?" He began pacing furiously, punctuating his words with angry stabs at the air. "I've spent every waking moment since we met proving myself to the great Laura Daniels. Did it ever occur to you that I might have doubts about *you?*"

"Like what?"

"Well, just look at you, Laura. Your whole life has been served up to you on a silver platter. You've never had to work for a damn thing."

"I've worked my—"

"Oh, yeah. You've put in some hours, sure. But you've never really *worked*—not the way I have. Worked to survive... Worked because if you didn't, you might never walk again." He stopped abruptly and turned to face her. "I've proved myself in ways you can't even begin to imagine. I don't have to prove anything to *you*."

The doorbell rang but Alex ignored it.

"You know, it's ironic." He laughed dryly. "You're obsessed with age—and you're the one who has to grow up. Life doesn't come in a neat box all tied up with a ribbon. It's tough and messy, and there aren't any guarantees. I'm ready to take the chance. But if you're not, tell me now."

Again the doorbell rang.

"You say you want me now—" she bit her lower lip "—but I'm only your first."

"First, twenty-first. What's the difference, Laura? I thought we were forever."

10

"WHAT?" Alex shouted in frustration as he threw open the door. A young Chinese man stood holding two paper bags. "Oh." Alex nodded, fishing in his pocket for money. He shoved a wad of bills at him. "Keep the change," he snapped, accepting the bags.

Now calm down, Alex. You're so mad, you just tipped that guy twenty bucks. He ignored his own advice, throwing the Chinese food onto a side table. Then he stormed back into the bedroom.

"Just what the hell set off this particular orgy of doubt, Laura?" he demanded.

"Nothing set it off," Laura shot back. "They are the normal doubts associated with this kind of relationship."

"*This* kind of relationship? What's that supposed to mean?"

Laura hesitated. "For crying out loud, Alex, the first man I slept with was older than me. He was in college and I was a high school girl and I was sure that was it. I was going to be with him forever—"

"There we go!" Alex pounced on her words. "You're the all-knowing older woman, I'm the naive high school boy. Hell, let's get it all out on the table. All right, Laura?" He began ticking off points on his fingers. "First, you're older. Thirteen years older. Second, you're my boss. Third, you make—I don't know—five times more money than I do? Fourth, and this is the real killer, you have made it professionally. While I—let's face it—am barely making a living as a musician." He made the word *musician* sound like something offensive. "You tell me, Laura. So what am I to you?"

Looking down at her hands, Laura was silent. Tears started falling from her eyes.

Alex moved closer, standing over her now. His voice lowered, he repeated the question. "So, what am I to you, Laura?"

"I think you're . . . a very gifted musician. Some of the people at work say you're a genius."

Alex nodded, waiting for more.

"And," Laura continued, fighting to control her sobs, "you're kind, sweet, thoughtful and . . . a wonderful lover. But . . ."

"But, what?"

Laura shook her head. "But you're so young. How can you make decisions that will last? You're just a—"

"Just a boy," Alex finished icily.

"No. No. Just . . . a young man."

For a long time both were silent. Finally Alex spoke. "Look at me," he said.

Laura kept her eyes lowered. Alex reached down to take her hand firmly in his own and pulled her upward till she met his gaze.

"Now you listen to me." His voice was so compelling that Laura felt it impossible to look away. The face she saw was hard, the eyes colder than she had ever imagined they could be. "I understand how you could have looked at me and seen all those nice—and *condescending*—things. 'Sweet,' I believe you said. 'Thoughtful.' 'Kind.' Yes, I hope I'm those things. And I hope that side of me is all I'll ever have to show to the world. I hope life allows me to be sweet and kind." His voice rose with anger. "But don't you *dare* to imagine that's all I am. Don't you *dare* to compare me to yourself as a schoolgirl.

"You're worried about people looking at you strangely because you're with me? And *you're* the strong one?" He laughed mirthlessly. "Laura, at my high school graduation, a year late, I was the guy in the goddamned wheelchair who the other kids wouldn't go near because the sight of me *scared* them. So spare me your tender sensibilities about what others may think when they see you with a younger man."

"I'm sorry," Laura whispered.

"And spare me your pity," Alex snapped. With one arm he drew her from the bed into his arms. His voice was a whisper now. "I grew up in hell, Laura, while you . . . Well, you grew up in Connecticut." He tightened his embrace. "And whatever my age, Laura, remember this: I am a man."

His kiss burned her lips.

With his right hand Alex unbuttoned her blouse and pulled it away. Then, with cool precision he unsnapped the closure of her bra. "I learn quickly," he said almost conversationally. "Shall I show you what else I've learned?"

Laura sagged against his chest. "Yes," she whispered, almost silently.

He took her then, satisfying his own need with her body. And when his final powerful thrust had carried Laura to a sobbing climax, he rose from her bed and dressed as she lay dazed and confused on crumpled sheets.

"Here," he said, pulling a Chinese fortune cookie from his shirt pocket and setting it on her nightstand. "Your future."

With that he turned and walked away. Only when she heard the front door close did Laura call out his name.

But there was no one left to hear her.

Much later, she broke open the cookie and found the diamond pendant, and turning it over, read the inscription through a blur of tears: *First and Forever.*

SOMEWHERE in a magazine once, Laura had seen a reference to the "domestic hum" of a busy household. The phrase had stuck with her, probably because of her notorious habit of humming at the most inopportune moments.

But it wasn't until Alex had disappeared from her life that she realized how quiet her life seemed without him. The domestic hum was gone, and an unnatural stillness pervaded every corner of her world.

She missed him most at night when her king-size bed felt as wide and empty as the ocean. She spent long nights in the company of her trusted notepad, compiling careful lists with headings like New Goals and Pros And Cons Of Calling Alex. She thought of making up a story that he was still desperately needed at the office, but he knew better than she that his work for the Universal account was complete. So she didn't arrive at any solution. But the lists were a good way to kill time. And she'd never had any success with counting sheep.

The days weren't much better. There were reminders of Alex everywhere. His toothbrush in the bathroom, for example. She'd bought him an extra when he started spending the night, and now that he was gone, she couldn't quite bring herself to throw it away. It sat there in her ceramic holder, a bright-blue symbol of her unhappiness.

There was sheet music on the piano. Cayenne pepper in her spice rack. Alex loved spicy food. The extra key he'd tossed on his way out the door. She'd begun to think of her co-op as the Alex and Laura Memorial Museum.

Still, Laura left everything just the way it was. Even if she could purge every single reminder of Alex, the persistent throb in her chest would be reminder enough.

She tried all the therapeutic interventions ever devised for a broken heart. She slaved away at work till late in the evening. She went to movies, sometimes with Rhoda, sometimes alone. She bought a new, indecently expensive dress at Bloomingdale's. And, in a last-ditch effort at self-help, she had a makeover done at La Coupe, a chic salon on Madison Avenue. She came out six hours and two hundred dollars later, looking very *vogue* and very unhappy. "Alex would hate it," she'd told Rhoda on the phone after her transformation.

"Wasn't that the idea?" Rhoda had prompted.

Well, yes and no. She'd hoped to reconnect with the woman she'd begun to think of as the "old" Laura—the soon-to-be-partner, woman-about-town Laura. But while the woman staring back at her in her dressing-room mirror was stunning, she wasn't at all the kind of woman who would jump in a New York cab at two in the morning, dressed only in a fur coat and high heels, with seduction on her mind.

"Face it, Laura," she told the woman in the mirror, "you've changed." She climbed into the shower and proceeded to wash two hundred dollars' worth of mousse and mascara down the drain.

THE DAY AFTER Laura's makeover disaster, Rhoda offered to buy her lunch. Laura had agreed, only to discover too late that Rhoda had developed an insatiable craving for nova lox. And what better place for smoked salmon, Rhoda had argued innocently, than Greene's deli?

"Humor me," she'd said. "I'm a hungry pregnant lady."

Laura had reluctantly agreed, but only after sending Rhoda ahead to make sure that Alex wasn't inside. Laura skulked out on Sixth Avenue, feeling idiotic, until Rhoda came back with the all clear.

"Why do I get the distinct impression you're disappointed Alex wasn't here?" Laura inquired as they scrambled for the last available table.

"Because I'm a romantic, and all romantics love a happy ending. Want to split a bagel?"

Laura frowned. Green's bagels held rather unhappy memories for her. "No. I'm not very hungry, anyway. I'll just have a salad."

"You're wasting away, you know," Rhoda chastised.

"Trust me. I'm in no immediate danger."

Rhoda leaned forward, as much as her belly would allow. "'Spose we *had* run into Alex? What would you have done?"

"Said polite hellos, I guess." Laura studied her menu energetically.

"Oh, Laura. You're so darn civilized."

"What would you have me do? I ask, incidentally," Laura added snidely, "because I'm sure you're going to tell me anyway."

"Jump his bones right here on this table. That's what," Rhoda said sharply.

Laura tossed her menu aside. "You know, ever since our breakup—for lack of a better term—you've been giving me not-so-subtle hints that you think I'm in the wrong."

"Moi?" Rhoda's jaw dropped open. "I value my life too much. No way."

"You're right. They haven't been subtle at all."

"I just hate to see things end this way. You two were perfect for each other." Rhoda cocked her head to one side, a faraway, melancholy look on her face.

"But we *weren't*, Rhoda. That's just the point." Once and for all, she was going to make Rhoda understand. "Just hear me out, okay?" she asked plaintively.

"I've been 'hearing you out' all week. And I still don't get it."

For the next ten minutes, Laura calmly presented her case again. Rhoda chewed on her bagel and lox, nodding intermittently but saying nothing.

When Laura finished, she waited for a response, feeling anxious and agitated. "Well?" she finally demanded.

Rhoda jerked up her head, looking for all the world like she'd just been roused from a satisfying nap.

"Well? Aren't you going to say anything?" Laura cried.

"You think Mrs. Greene has any fresh decaf made?"

"I just bared my soul to you and you want to know about decaffeinated coffee?" Laura's voice rose above the noisy din of the restaurant.

"Perhaps you should try it." Rhoda patted Laura's hand. "Besides, that's the tenth time this week you've bared your soul to me. Nothing personal, but your soul and I have filled our 'quality time' quota for the foreseeable future. Besides, Laura, if you have to try this hard to convince people you're right, it kind of seems to me that you're mostly trying to convince yourself. And I can't help you there."

Laura slumped in her seat, defeated. It was quite possible Rhoda was right.

"I'm sorry," she apologized. "I must have sounded like a pretty big crybaby lately."

"That's okay." Rhoda chuckled. "Wait till you see me during labor. I'm planning on being a real pain in the butt. Although it turns out you may be spared that chore. Did I tell you that Rick got his leave?"

"Hey, that's terrific."

"It starts the fourteenth, the day before my due date, which is cutting it a bit close if you ask me, but it's four full weeks, so maybe the almighty Navy has a heart, after all." She finished off her bagel and said dryly, "Now, all I have to do is hold out till the big day."

"That reminds me—" Laura reached for her purse and fished inside. "Look what I got for us." She handed Rhoda a small black box with a belt clip on it. "It's a beeper. So if you need me when I'm say, stuck in line at Bloomie's or something, I can rush to your rescue." She wrote the number on a slip of paper and handed it to Rhoda.

"You're incredible." Rhoda shook her head, giving Laura a grateful smile. "What would I do without you?"

Laura rolled her eyes toward the ceiling. "Anybody who's put up with me these past few days deserves a medal. You're the incredible one."

The waitress dropped the check on their table and Rhoda went to grab it. "Allow me," Laura insisted. "As of Monday I will be a partner, after all. I guess."

"P-Day, that's right. You excited?"

Laura looked away pensively. "Strangely enough, no." She shrugged, deliberately brightening. "Maybe it's just a delayed reaction."

"Very delayed," Rhoda added. "Guess you'll really be one of the Beautiful People now, huh?"

"Yep. Me and Donald Trump," Laura said laconically. Laura hesitated. Should she tell Rhoda? Well, yes, she pretty much had to, sooner or later. She might as well get it over with. "Margo Morgenroth called."

"Oh, *did* she?" Rhoda marveled. "Did you let her have it?"

"No." Laura looked away.

"Oh, no. Don't tell me . . ."

Laura shrugged helplessly. "She promised me. I mean, she swore up and down this guy was great. Besides, his name's Gary Weiss. A nice, normal, unpretentious name. How bad can he be?"

"I think after J. Parke, you know just how bad he can be."

"Now, don't give me that disapproving look," Laura said defensively. "I have to get on with my life. Besides, I set the date up for the Four Seasons again. The maître d' there kind of knows the routine by now."

"I don't think Alex is going to rescue you twice, Laura."

"Won't have to." Laura held up the electronic pager. "I'll just have you beep me, and I'm outta there."

A FEW HOURS LATER, Laura found herself listlessly toying with yet another salad in yet another deli. Only this time she was in the village, just a stone's throw from Mickey-O's. And this time, Rhoda hadn't dragged her here. She'd come all on her own.

Ostensibly she was here for some career counseling. The question, as Laura saw it, was fairly straightforward. She had two choices, and two more days to make up her mind. And whichever choice she made would forever alter the course of her life.

There was option one, the one everyone figured was a shoo-in. A million-dollar-a-year partnership in one of the biggest advertising agencies in the most exciting city on earth. When she put it that way, it did have a certain je ne sais quoi, didn't it?

Then there was option number two. The dark-horse candidate. Hanging out a shingle in some godforsaken backwater, writing ad copy for *Fertilizer Monthly*.

She stabbed at a cherry tomato. The choice did seem rather obvious. So why was she drawn to option two? With instincts like this, was it any wonder she was unlucky in love? She always went for the long shots.

From the moment Larry had mentioned the word *partner* on Gordy's boat, only Alex had sensed her doubts. He knew the partnership represented the safe choice, the easy victory. And only he knew just what she was afraid of: the possibility that if she struck out on her own, she might fail.

She caught herself just the other day looking out of her office window toward Alex's apartment across the street, wondering what advice he'd give her. But he'd had the blinds drawn most of the time lately. In a way she was thankful not to have to catch sight of him that way. She wasn't sure she was that strong, yet. But if missing him physically wasn't bad enough, she also missed his advice and counsel. He always seemed to know what was right for her.

The night of her birthday he'd told her just that. Suddenly she realized why it had been true. Alex always seemed to want her to do what was hardest, even if it meant she might fail. He believed in her. Believed in her enough to advise challenge over security.

In the cellar across the way, Mickey-O's would be rumbling to life right around now. Alex would be at the piano, filling the room with sounds that made you want to cry.

Her own life had been far too quiet lately. And maybe even a little too easy.

It was time to start doing the hard things. She paid her bill and headed for Mickey-O's.

ALEX GOT UP from the piano, shoving the bench back and almost knocking it over. He left the stage, barely acknowledging the applause of the crowd.

Pity applause, he thought sardonically. Some in the audience just didn't know enough about music to realize how bad he was; and the others were being kind. But the guys in the band had been giving him looks lately. Looks that said: "Hey, boy, we're carrying you."

They were carrying him. He'd missed cues all night, not to mention rolling right over part of the trumpet solo. He was playing like an amateur.

Alex sagged against the bar, letting his head drop until his forehead rested on the varnished mahogany.

"Bad night, Alex, my man?" The bartender always put the emphasis on the last syllable of his name.

"I sucked," Alex replied, raising his head. "Dewey, I need a drink."

"That ain't your problem." The bartender laughed. "You got that *other* problem. And no drink's gonna fix woman trouble. I know. I've tried."

"Bourbon," Alex said. "Isn't that the preferred drink of jazzmen?"

"Mmm-hmm." Dewey nodded dubiously. "Soda pop, the preferred drink of the smart ones." But he poured Alex a shot of Jack Daniels.

Alex tossed it down in a swallow, then coughed, gasping for air. "Man, that's terrible. Why didn't you warn me? Stuff could kill you."

"Most folks drink it a bit slower," Dewey commented dryly, moving off to tend to other customers.

Well, Alex thought, so much for drowning my sorrows—at least, with bourbon. Besides, the problem was he just couldn't seem to concentrate on the music, and he couldn't see where getting smashed would help.

"Mind if I join you?"

Alex looked up to see Becky taking the stool next to him. The dark-haired waitress flashed a smile and began extracting a cigarette from her purse.

"Aren't you supposed to be working?"

"I'm on break," Becky said, lighting her cigarette. "How you been?" She looked at him speculatively.

"How do I sound?" Alex countered rhetorically.

"I don't mean your music. I meant you. How have you been?"

Alex shrugged. "The usual. Fine."

"Rumor has it you broke up with that woman." Becky cast him a sidelong glance, waiting for his answer.

"That woman?" Alex repeated dully. "Yeah. I guess I broke up with that woman."

"What was her name? Like, Margaret or something?"

No, Alex answered silently. It was Laura. Laura. But he couldn't bring himself to say her name out loud. "Yeah, Margaret," he told her, his voice edged with anger.

"Thought so," Becky agreed. She took another puff, then, her voice all careful nonchalance, said, "You know, I live just a few blocks away."

"Uh-huh?" he inquired disinterestly.

"And my roommate's gone to visit her mom in Indiana, so I have the place all to myself." She waited vainly for Alex's response. "You could come over after the last set. You know, listen to music." She turned to look directly into his eyes. "And whatever else you want."

"What?" Alex shook his head, as though suddenly aware that she was there.

Becky pulled a slip of paper from her purse and stuffed it slowly into his pants pockets. "That's my address. I'll be out of here before you tonight. Dara has the late shift. But . . . If you were to drop by after you get off . . . Well, that would be nice."

"Oh. Umm, thanks." He was completely nonplussed. She was actually coming on to him. Becky. What a strange notion.

"Play something for me, all right?" Becky made a kissing gesture, and stubbed out her cigarette. "Well, back to the grindstone."

Alex was still at a loss, watching her walk away. Out of the corner of his eye, he caught Dewey shaking his head slowly, obviously amused.

Back at the piano, his surprise gradually shifted into resentment. What he did not need at this particular moment in his life was someone making him even more uncomfortable. What on earth made Becky think... Wasn't it obvious that he was still far from being free of Laura?

He struck the opening chords of "The Memphis Blues" almost angrily. Across the room he could see Becky, standing by a table taking an order. Yes, she was attractive, he supposed. Odd, but he'd never really noticed. Yes, by most standards she was pretty. But the thought of being with her—well, it just seemed wrong.

As wrong as the note he'd just struck. He shot the trumpet player a look that said "Sorry."

There had been a time—a very recent time—when, he supposed, an invitation to the apartment of a pretty girl would have seemed . . . Well, it would have scared him. Still, he could imagine that at some other point in life he might have found Becky attractive.

Before Laura.

Now? He labored his way through a complex passage. *Now, in the world after Laura?*

He shook his head. There was no world after Laura.

The tune ended and he looked up, managing a sad smile, to see Becky watching.

All right, Alex. Play her a song. And then, go home alone. As usual.

He leaned down to the keyboard microphone and said, "This is for a friend of mine. Becky, I know you like this tune."

He eased into a slow rendition of "My Funny Valentine," and thanked providence that he at least hadn't screwed up the introduction. But a movement out in the dark beyond the fog of colored lights caught his eye. He squinted and made out just the back of her head as she disappeared.

Laura.

He raced through the rest of the song, manhandling the tune. And as soon as the last key was struck, Alex ran from the stage. He was halfway out the door when he heard Danny Oransky beside him and felt the man's hand on his shoulder.

"She's gone, Alex."

Alex spun away and slammed a fist against the wall. "Damn it!"

"Saw her catch a cab," Oransky said. "Didn't look like a happy woman."

"Yeah," Alex replied bitterly. "Well, that makes two of us." He seethed, biting his lip before calming enough to apologize. "Sorry, Danny. I'm not myself."

"You haven't been yourself for a while. I'm sorry to say it, Alex, but the music is suffering."

Alex closed his eyes and slumped against the wall. "You gonna fire me?"

"No."

"'Cause if you did, I couldn't blame you."

"I'm not going to fire you, Alex," Oransky answered kindly. Then his voice hardened. "But, old and skinny as I am, I'm gonna kick your butt if you screw up and let that woman get away."

"What can I do?" Alex questioned bleakly. "It was her decision."

"'What can I do?'" Oransky mimicked. "'It was her decision'? What happened to you, boy? When did you start letting anything, let alone a few angry words, keep you from what you want?"

Alex looked up, puzzled.

"I thought you were a badass, Alex. I thought you were the guy nothing could stop. And now it's 'What can I do?' Whining and moping around here and screwing up the music." Oransky laughed, clearly trying to provoke a response. "Are you really Alex, or are you his weeny twin?"

Alex smiled reluctantly. He looked at Oransky and nodded. "'Weeny twin,' huh?" He stood and felt the confused haze lift like a fog in the sunshine. "Danny, let me tell you something, and mark my words. I am going to marry that annoying, irritating woman. Whether she likes it or not. But right now," he turned back toward the stage, "you'd better nail down the breakables, old man, 'cause I'm going to play some music."

LAURA SPENT the next twenty-four hours totally numb. It was like getting a dose of Novocain: She knew that when the stuff wore off, she was going to hurt like crazy; but for the time being, nothing much seemed to matter.

And after all, was it really such a shock that Alex had proved her right? True, he hadn't wasted any time replacing her—and, she would have hoped for someone a little less, say, *young*, than Becky. But it really wasn't her place to quibble.

Laura checked her watch. Yes, it was time. Time to go out and have fun. Good luck to poor Mr. Weiss, getting stuck with her tonight.

She went to her bedroom and began dressing with all the enthusiasm of a zombie. She wore exactly what she had for the last Margo date—sexy black dress and diamond earrings—but with none of her previous anticipation. This time she fully expected disaster. That realization had an oddly calming effect on her nerves. What did it matter? What did anything matter?

As she gazed at her reflection in the mirror, she realized how lovely Alex's pendant would look with her earrings. She'd thought about returning it to him, but had been unable to release it. Trying it on now was strictly an aesthetic decision, not an emotional one, but when she fastened the chain around her throat, she experienced the first sharp pang in her chest—the first thing she'd felt all day. Apparently the "Novocain" was wearing off.

Laura tried to remember why she was going on this date. Something about helping her to get over Alex, wasn't it? She ran her fingers over the diamonds at her throat and gulped back the threat of tears. It was too late to back out now, for heaven's sake. Just go and get it over with. Eat, drink and be miserable.

WHEN LAURA ARRIVED by cab at the Four Seasons a few minutes late, the maître d' took one look at her and blossomed into what was—for all appearances—a sincere smile. *"Madame!"* he enthused, rushing to greet her. "How delightful to see you again."

"What can I say?" Laura muttered. "I'm a glutton for punishment."

"I hope this evening will prove more, shall we say, productive, than your last visit."

"Don't count on it." She glanced around, wondering vaguely how she would recognize her date. On second thought, that shouldn't be too tough—just look for the most obnoxious guy in the place.

"Your date has already arrived," the maître d' said, answering her question before she could ask it. "Please, follow me."

"Wait." Laura clutched the man's arm. She reached into her purse and pulled out a card with a number written on the back. "This is my beeper number. If this one is like the last one . . ."

The maître d' smiled and accepted the card. "I suspect I shall not need this."

She followed behind him for only a few more steps before he stood aside. "Your table, *madame*."

Laura braced herself, plastered a smile on her face and looked up to see her date.

The smile faltered and faded as she saw him rise to greet her.

Her date was Alex.

11

LAURA STOOD motionless. Apparently her shoes had been glued to the floor. Not unlike the mask of shock permanently plastered on her face.

"Madame?" the maître d' prompted. "Your table?" He extended his arm in Alex's direction.

Alex walked over to her, moving with an easy, masculine confidence. His smile was so subtle, only she could possibly perceive it. But it was there, all right. There was no doubt in her mind that Alex was very definitely enjoying himself.

She held out her hand. "Mr. Weiss, I presume."

Alex grasped her hand and lavished it with a lingering kiss. "Mr. Weiss was the recipient of an urgent phone call informing him you'd be unable to make it this evening. You sent profuse apologies."

"Well," Laura managed, "I'm glad I was polite, at least." She started to say more, but her mouth was suddenly very dry. Long moments trudged past. *What game are we playing?* Laura wondered. *What does this man want?*

Alex broke the silence. "Sorry about your date, but he wasn't right for you. Guess we'll just have to make the best of it." He placed his hand at the small of her back. "You'd better sit down. You look a little pale."

She allowed herself to be led to the table and sat down woodenly.

"Will there be anything else, sir?" the maître d' asked as Alex took his seat.

"No, thank you, Maurice. You've been a big help." Laura could have sworn she saw Alex wink. The maître d' gave a little bow and departed.

"Maurice?" Laura echoed incredulously.

Alex shrugged. "We go way back." He reached across the table, brushing his fingers across her hand. "Great dress, by the way." His gaze dropped to her low-cut bodice and the diamond glittering at her throat. "Great necklace, too."

What on earth had possessed her to wear it tonight, of all nights? "It matches my earrings," she mumbled lamely.

"So it does." Alex moved his hand away and crossed his arms over his chest. "A gift?"

She could see he was in his "anthropologist" phase now, eyeing her with cool, almost clinical, detachment. Laura nodded tersely. She really didn't like this game. "Birthday."

"Would there be an inscription?"

That did it. "Alex," Laura demanded, fighting back the overpowering urge to hurl a piece of very expensive china at him, "why are you here? I mean, where are we going with all this?"

Alex pointed a finger at her. "*Exactly* my question. And after careful consideration, I can see only one solution."

His irritating grin was making homicide a very real possibility. "Well?" she grated.

"Well," he said, blushing a little. "Marriage, obviously."

Her heart clutched in her chest. "Marriage to *who*?"

"Whom, Laura. Why, to me, of course. Was there someone else in the running?"

Shock gave way to fury. It was time to bring out the big guns. "Well, off the top of my head, your little friend Becky comes to mind."

Alex did not even blink. He waved to Maurice, who appeared at their tableside almost instantly, carrying a bottle of Dom Perignon.

"The champagne you requested, Mr. Shaw," said the maître d'.

"Don't you have anything else to do?" Laura inquired frostily. This evening had "conspiracy" written all over it.

"I've taken a certain professional interest in this table, *madame*," Maurice explained. He opened the champagne, awaiting Alex's approval.

"How nice," Laura said evenly.

Alex nodded, and when the maître d' had finished pouring, he disappeared as discreetly as he'd appeared.

"I think a toast is in order, don't you?" Alex asked, lifting his glass. He cleared his throat. "To marital bliss."

Laura didn't move.

"No? Okay, I get it. We'll work up to that one gradually." He didn't seem to expect a reply. Suddenly he snapped his fingers. "I've got it. We never really formally celebrated your partnership. I mean, we did the Mickey-O's scene, but with all deference to my employer, that crowd can get awfully rowdy. And of course, the service is so much better here." He gave Laura a meaningful, you-needn't-bring-her-up-again look. "So, to—"

"Do you dedicate songs to all the waitresses there?" Laura interrupted.

"Most of them, at one point or another." Alex nodded. "But I only *write* songs for you." He hummed a few notes to himself. "You know, I think there's a good lyric in there, somewhere. But—" he shrugged "—what do I care? My jingle-writing days are over."

"What?" Laura scoffed. "You can write your own ticket, after the Universal ads start coming out."

"Naw." He wrinkled his nose. "Nothing personal, but that Tate and O'Neill crowd's too stuffy for my taste."

"Knock on any door on Madison Avenue, Alex. Don't be dumb. They'll be tripping all over themselves to give you work. There are creative directors who'd just love to get their hands on you." Alex raised his brows suggestively, and she dropped her gaze. "You know what I mean," Laura said.

"Yeah, I guess you're right. And I hate to say you told me so, but I kind of do think advertising's a gas. Jazz or jingle, I guess you're communicating an idea or a feeling musically. And—" he shook his head regretfully "—it's a helluva lot better money."

Laura sighed. "Alex," she began, then stopped herself. Was he being facetious or was this the way he truly felt? And more to the point, was he just saying these things because he thought she needed to hear them? "Alex," she began again, "I don't want to keep playing this game. I don't want to banter and be witty with you. I need to know how you really feel. I need to know what you really want—not what you think will make me happy. Because I could never be happy if I thought I had led you to change—to give up any part of your dreams for me."

Alex nodded. "You're right. But I want so many things. And sometimes those things conflict. Sometimes it's hard to know what order to take things in." He smiled. "I may be wise beyond my tender years but that doesn't mean I have all the answers at my fingertips. But here goes." He leaned forward and looked straight into her eyes, looked away for a moment, then returned his gaze to her, this time unwavering. "I want you, Laura. That's number one, because if I don't have you, then I don't have anything that matters. You are the necessary ingredient. You are the prerequisite for joy in my life. You are the beginning. And everything else that I want—everything else that I dream of in life—will only have meaning if you're there."

He sat back, his face wearing a wistful smile. "Would I give up everything else in my life to be with you? Yes. I would. And count myself lucky in the bargain. But—" he smiled wryly "—I really don't think anything quite that dramatic is going to be necessary. Because I have a question for you now, and I think I already know the answer."

"What question?" Laura asked softly.

"What do *you* want?" Alex replied softly. "Or, to be more specific, are you going to take that partnership?"

Laura was silent for a while, looking down at the table. Then she began to shake her head slowly from side to side. "You piss me off, Alex."

"And why is that?" He grinned.

"'Cause I don't like the fact that you know what I want before I know what I want. How am I going to live with you?" She laughed softly. "No. No, I'm not going to take that partnership. And yes, despite the fact that I'm still mad at you, although I don't remember why anymore, I love you with all my heart. And if I'm sure of nothing else, I'm sure of that."

"People may look at us funny, may think I'm your 'kept' man, you know."

"Yeah?" Laura shot back. "Then they're just jealous."

"I'll probably have to be out late playing. Several nights a week," Alex cautioned. "I mean, man does not live by jingles alone."

Laura pointed a finger at him. "You just stay away from the waitresses, and dedicate all your songs to me."

"Deal." Alex nodded. "This will make things much easier, because just in case you gave me any trouble tonight, I was prepared to kidnap— What the hell was that?" He looked at her strangely.

The electronic chirp sounded again. "Oh, it's this beeper I got. I was going to have your friend Maurice get me out of this if you . . . I mean, if the unfortunate Mr. Weiss was a creep. It's basically for Rhoda when . . . when . . ." Her jaw dropped open. "Oh, no."

Alex turned to the maître d'. "You guys have a phone?"

Something in the pale look on Alex's face motivated Maurice to snap his fingers for a busboy, sending him an urgent signal.

"Now, it's probably nothing, Laura," Alex reassured her, feeling none too sure himself.

"No, no, it's too early. It's weeks till . . ." She looked up at Alex with an almost-comical expression of horror. "I can't do this."

The maître d' handed her the portable phone. She tried the number twice before managing to dial correctly.

Rhoda answered on the fifth ring.

"Laura, that you?"

"Oh, my God," Laura said.

"Listen, I hate to put a damper on the festivities . . . Wait a minute, you two *are* back together by now, aren't you?"

"Why aren't you at the hospital?"

"Well, I didn't want to interrupt." Rhoda laughed.

"Stop worrying about my love life and get to the hospital!" Laura demanded.

"Is there a love life to worry about?"

"Yes, already!" Laura shouted in exasperation.

"Okay, then. In that case, I'll have the baby," Rhoda said matter-of-factly.

"Oh, my God," Laura repeated.

"Laura, give me Alex."

Laura held the phone out to Alex. "She wants to talk to you."

Alex looked startled, but took the receiver. "Uh-huh." He smiled and nodded assent. "I'll do that, but you get your butt into a cab or Laura's going to hyperventilate. See you in a few minutes. Bye." He turned to Laura. "She made me promise to do something to you before I let you go."

"What? Anything!"

"Drink your champagne, then. She made me promise to pour a good stiff drink down you." Alex laughed. "I think she somehow got the impression you were frazzled."

Laura grabbed her glass and emptied it in a gulp. "Let's call a cab."

"Let's take my limo."

"Your what?"

Alex shrugged. "I missed my senior prom—what can I say? Besides, I had other uses in mind for it, but it will get us to the hospital on time."

They made a dash for the exit. At the curb Alex summoned a long gray Lincoln with a wave of his hand. Without waiting for the driver to open their door, they piled in. "Mount Sinai Hospital, Hal, and punch it." He winced at the sound of his own words.

The big car blasted off from the curb, slamming them back against their seats.

"If this doesn't cure you of your speed paranoia," Laura whispered breathlessly, "nothing will."

Alex laughed shakily. "Tinted glass," he pointed at the darkened windows. "I'm hoping what I can't see won't hurt me."

ALEX HAD NEVER LIKED hospitals, having spent far too much time inside them, but six hours into this "baby" vigil he'd discovered a whole new reason to hate them.

"This has got to be the worst coffee on the planet," he griped to a rumpled-looking waiting-room comrade. He set aside the grayish brew and picked up the same *Field and Stream* magazine he'd read front to back hours earlier. "You know, I wouldn't mind reading this magazine a second time," he continued for the benefit of anyone in earshot, "if it weren't already a year and a half old."

"Must be your first kid, huh?" the rumpled man asked. He was a good ten years older than Alex, with a scruffy beard growth and deep blue hollows beneath his weary eyes.

"Yes." Alex nodded. "In a manner of speaking. Is it always this much fun?"

The man rolled his jacket into a makeshift pillow and stretched out on the orange vinyl couch next to Alex's chair. "Could be worse. We could be in there with 'em. Me, I don't believe in this natural-childbirth baloney. I mean, I'm sorry, but I ain't gonna go in there. Not in this lifetime, pal. And since you're out here, I guess you agree."

"Actually, my girlfriend's in there with the mother—" Alex stopped himself too late.

"Yeah?" The man chuckled. "Kid, you're gonna burn yourself out before you're thirty, but hey, more power to you."

Alex buried his nose in the magazine, hoping to buy himself some peace from any further conversation about his love life. He consulted his watch. Hal, the limo driver, was charging a small hourly fortune, but Alex had asked him to stick around. How long did this labor stuff take, anyway? He considered asking his new acquaintance, then decided against further contact. Instead, he cracked his knuckles, trying to disperse some of the tension threatening to tie him into knots. Lord, he hoped Rhoda was okay.

He wondered, assuming everything went well, if Laura would be in any frame of mind to pursue his little plan. Today it had seemed brilliant. Breathtaking, even. Tonight it seemed...well, like an impetuous long shot. But, he'd gone this far. He really had no choice but to go for broke—

"It's a girl!"

Alex looked up to see Laura explode through the double doors, looking flushed and dewy-eyed.

"And Rhoda?" he asked, rushing to hug her.

"Terrific, wonderful! But, boy, she knows some interesting words." She embraced Alex happily. "And guess what she's naming the baby?"

"Rickette?"

"No, silly. Laura!" she exclaimed. "After me."

"That would follow." Alex laughed. "Can I see them?"

"Rhoda's passed out. I think she might be a little tired. Six hours of heavy breathing and calisthenics will do that, I guess. We can see her again tomorrow—wait—it *is* tomorrow, isn't it?"

"You tired?" Alex asked, trying to keep the anticipation out of his voice.

"Are you kidding? I'm going to have a goddaughter." She laughed happily. "I look pretty bad, probably, but I'm way too wired to sleep."

"Well, I have the limo for a while longer." Alex slid his hands down to her hips and eased her closer. "It doesn't turn into a pumpkin till dawn. And there's something I wanted to show you."

"Oh, really?" Laura smiled suggestively. "I'm all yours, Prince Charming."

"That's what I'm hoping." Alex took her hand and led her toward the elevator, then turned to call to his fellow father-in-waiting: "Hey, good luck, man!"

"You too, kid," he answered with a tired wave. "You're gonna need it more than me."

"What was that all about?" Laura inquired as they waited for an elevator.

"Long story. You know, it ain't easy being a father, I've discovered."

"Yeah, right," Laura said, rolling her eyes. "Snoozing on the couch, reading magazines. That can take a lot out of you, poor baby. Labor, on the other hand, is a breeze. That's why they call it labor."

"Oh, I see," Alex joked as they entered the elevator. "Now I'm going to have to hear all about suffering womanhood. But really, how was it? How'd you hold up?"

"Oh, you'll be relieved to hear I acquitted myself reasonably well. Once I got in there the boss in me took over, I guess." She smiled proudly. "This know-it-all resident started giving Rhoda a hard time because she felt like walking around a bit. I straightened him out, shall we say."

"Any physical violence?"

"No more than necessary." They arrived at the ground floor and strolled toward the hospital parking area. Laura laced her fingers through Alex's and sighed contentedly. "I wish you could have seen little Laura," she mused. "She's a knockout."

Alex gave a low whistle.

"She was beautiful. Squished-up little red face and tons of dark hair." She sighed again. "Beautiful. I felt . . . wonderful, being a part of it all." She stopped, cocking her head while she gave Alex careful scrutiny. "If I ever had a baby, would you be my coach?"

She wasn't inviting as much as doubting his moral fiber, Alex figured. "Laura, there's a way things are done," he mimicked from a conversation of not so long ago. "First you need a husband and wife, see?"

They arrived at the limo and she decided to let the answer slide. Hal opened the door and they settled into the back seat. Laura snuggled against Alex's shoulder unselfconsciously.

"Where to?" the driver asked.

"That address I gave you earlier," Alex answered conspiratorially.

"Punch it, sir?"

"No. Nice and slow." Alex laughed.

"Now I'm curious," Laura murmured, rubbing her cheek against the nubby fabric of his jacket. "Where are we going?"

"To a place you've only dreamed about." Alex's tone was intriguing.

"You've already done that," Laura answered huskily.

Alex surprised her with a fierce kiss. Until that very second she hadn't known how desperately she'd longed for his touch. She responded to him gratefully, drinking in the pleasure of it.

When at last they parted, Laura glanced up to see the driver through the open partition, smiling at them in his rearview mirror. She nudged Alex, and they laughed softly.

For the rest of the trip they nestled in each other's arms.

"You know," Laura whispered, running her fingers along the dense muscles of Alex's thigh, "it's strange. We haven't really settled anything. All our problems are still there, waiting for solutions, and yet, somehow, I feel wonderful. In fact, I've never been happier."

"I have a theory," Alex replied. "Sometimes when you stop trying to control your world every waking minute, things just have a way of magically falling into place."

"Maybe so." Laura planted a tiny kiss on his earlobe. "All I know is, I saw that baby make her debut onto this planet, and all I could think was *Yes. This is what it's all about. This is all that matters.*" She wiped away a tear. "Profound, huh?"

Alex pulled her into a long, silent embrace. "Very," he whispered.

A few moments later the limousine decreased speed. Laura lowered her window and gasped. "Wait a minute." She turned to Alex, who was a study in nonchalance. "We're in Connecticut."

"No kidding," Alex observed. "Time flies."

"I've always loved this town. It's perfectly charming," Laura continued. "Have you ever been to this area?"

"Once or twice." He had suddenly taken a decided interest in the portable-bar gadgetry.

The limo rounded a corner and slowed to a stop before a lovely red-brick turn-of-the-century home. A massive elm dominated the front yard, which was illuminated by a bright gaslight, and flower beds lined the slate walkway leading to a broad front porch. A big, boisterous dog romped back and forth, reined in only by a white fence that rimmed the property.

A white picket fence.

"Here we are," Hal announced.

Laura stopped making any effort to breathe. She didn't want to think what she was thinking, for fear she might be wrong. "Alex?" she ventured in a hoarse whisper.

He shrugged casually. "It's available, if we want it. Of course, we'd have to bring our own dog."

She still hadn't breathed. "What are you saying?"

"I'm saying that I talked to the realtor today and it's still available. It's zoned commercial, so you could set up shop right here, if you wanted. And it's close enough for me to still play weekend gigs at Mickey-O's." He didn't want to know what she was thinking for fear he might be wrong. "There's room for my piano, and for those hideous couches of yours, if you really insist, and—" he looked away "—and there's room for a nursery."

At last she breathed. "You do understand," she said with a radiant smile, "that when I'm, say, seventy, you'll only be fifty-seven?"

Alex only smiled in answer. "Drive on," he instructed Hal.

"Where to?" the driver asked.

"Doesn't matter," Alex answered softly. He shut the glass partition behind Hal, giving them complete privacy, and pulled Laura into his arms. "After all, we've got all the time in the world."

"Yes, love," Laura whispered back. "We've got forever."

PENNY JORDAN

Sins and infidelities . . .
Dreams and obsessions . . .
Shattering secrets
unfold in . . .

THE HIDDEN YEARS

SAGE — stunning, sensual and vibrant, she spent a lifetime distancing herself from a past too painful to confront . . . the mother who seemed to hold her at bay, the father who resented her and the heartache of unfulfilled love. To the world, Sage was independent and invulnerable— but it was a mask she cultivated to hide a desperation she herself couldn't quite understand . . . until an unforeseen turn of events drew her into the discovery of the hidden years, finally allowing Sage to open her heart to a passion denied for so long.

The Hidden Years—a compelling novel of truth and passion that will unlock the heart and soul of every woman.

AVAILABLE IN OCTOBER!
Watch for your opportunity to complete your Penny Jordan set.
POWER PLAY and SILVER will also be available in October.

HARLEQUIN
Romance®

**This September, travel to England
with Harlequin Romance
FIRST CLASS title #3149,
ROSES HAVE THORNS
by Betty Neels**

It was Radolf Nauta's fault that Sarah lost her job at the hospital and was forced to look elsewhere for a living. So she wasn't particulary pleased to meet him again in a totally different environment. Not that he seemed disposed to be gracious to her: arrogant, opinionated and entirely too sure of himself, Radolf was just the sort of man Sarah disliked most. And yet, the more she saw of him, the more she found herself wondering what he really thought about her—which was stupid, because he was the last man on earth she could ever love....

MILLION DOLLAR JACKPOT
SWEEPSTAKES RULES & REGULATIONS
NO PURCHASE NECESSARY TO ENTER OR RECEIVE A PRIZE

1 Alternate means of entry: Print your name and address on a 3" x 5" piece of plain paper and send to the appropriate address below.

In the U.S.	**In Canada**
MILLION DOLLAR JACKPOT	MILLION DOLLAR JACKPOT
P.O. Box 1867	P.O. Box 609
3010 Walden Avenue	Fort Erie, Ontario
Buffalo, NY 14269-1867	L2A 5X3

2. To enter the Sweepstakes and join the Reader Service, check off the "YES" box on your Sweepstakes Entry Form and return. If you do not wish to join the Reader Service but wish to enter the Sweepstakes only, check off the "NO" box on your Sweepstakes Entry Form. To qualify for the Extra Bonus prize, scratch off the silver on your Lucky Keys. If the registration numbers match, you are eligible for the Extra Bonus Prize offering. Incomplete entries are ineligible. Torstar Corp. and its affiliates are not responsible for mutilated or unreadable entries or inadvertent printing errors. Mechanically reproduced entries are null and void.

3. Whether you take advantage of this offer or not, on or about April 30, 1992, at the offices of D.L. Blair, Inc., Blair, NE, your sweepstakes numbers will be compared against the list of winning numbers generated at random by the computer. However, prizes will only be awarded to individuals who have entered the Sweepstakes. In the event that all prizes are not claimed, a random drawing will be held from all qualified entries received from March 30, 1990 to March 31, 1992, to award all unclaimed prizes. All cash prizes (Grand to Sixth) will be mailed to winners and are payable by check in U.S. funds. Seventh Prize will be shipped to winners via third-class mail. These prizes are in addition to any free, surprise or mystery gifts that might be offered. Versions of this Sweepstakes with different prizes of approximate equal value may appear at retail outlets or in other mailings by Torstar Corp. and its affiliates.

4. PRIZES: (1) *Grand Prize $1,000,000.00 Annuity; (1) First Prize $25,000.00; (1) Second Prize $10,000.00; (5) Third Prize $5,000.00; (10) Fourth Prize $1,000.00; (100) Fifth Prize $250.00; (2,500) Sixth Prize $10.00; (6,000) **Seventh Prize $12.95 ARV.

    *This presentation offers a Grand Prize of a $1,000,000.00 annuity. Winner will receive $33,333.33 a year for 30 years without interest totalling $1,000,000.00.

    **Seventh Prize: A fully illustrated hardcover book, published by Torstar Corp. Approximate Retail Value of the book is $12.95.

    Entrants may cancel the Reader Service at any time without cost or obligation (see details in Center Insert Card).

5. Extra Bonus! This presentation offers an Extra Bonus Prize valued at $33,000.00 to be awarded in a random drawing from all qualified entries received by March 31, 1992. No purchase necessary to enter or receive a prize. To qualify, see instructions in Center Insert Card. Winner will have the choice of any of the merchandise offered or a $33,000.00 check payable in U.S. funds. All other published rules and regulations apply.

6. This Sweepstakes is being conducted under the supervision of D.L. Blair, Inc. By entering the Sweepstakes, each entrant accepts and agrees to be bound by these rules and the decisions of the judges, which shall be final and binding. Odds of winning the random drawing are dependent upon the number of entries received. Taxes, if any, are the sole responsibility of the winners. Prizes are nontransferable. All entries must be received at the address on the detachable Business Reply Card and must be postmarked no later than 12:00 MIDNIGHT on March 31, 1992. The drawing for all unclaimed Sweepstakes prizes and for the Extra Bonus Prize will take place on May 30, 1992, at 12:00 NOON at the offices of D.L. Blair, Inc., Blair, NE.

7. This offer is open to residents of the U.S., United Kingdom, France and Canada, 18 years or older, except employees and immediate family members of Torstar Corp., its affiliates, subsidiaries and all other agencies, entities and persons connected with the use, marketing or conduct of this Sweepstakes. All Federal, State, Provincial, Municipal and local laws apply. Void wherever prohibited or restricted by law. Any litigation within the Province of Quebec respecting the conduct and awarding of a prize in this publicity contest must be submitted to the Régie des Loteries et Courses du Québec.

8. Winners will be notified by mail and may be required to execute an affidavit of eligibility and release, which must be returned within 14 days after notification or an alternate winner may be selected. Canadian winners will be required to correctly answer an arithmetical, skill-testing question administered by mail, which must be returned within a limited time. Winners consent to the use of their name, photograph and/or likeness for advertising and publicity in conjunction with this and similar promotions without additional compensation.

9. For a list of our major prize winners, send a stamped, self-addressed envelope to: MILLION DOLLAR WINNERS LIST, P.O. Box 4510, Blair, NE 68009. Winners Lists will be supplied after the May 30, 1992 drawing date.

Offer limited to one per household.

LTY-H891

Coming Soon

Fashion A Whole New You
in classic romantic style
with a trip for two to Paris
via American Airlines®, a
brand-new Mercury Sable
LS and a $2,000 Fashion
Allowance.

Plus, romantic free gifts* are yours to
Fashion A Whole New You.

From September through November, you can take part in
this exciting opportunity from Harlequin.

Watch for details in September.

* with proofs-of-purchase, plus postage and handling

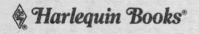 *Harlequin Books*®

HQFW-TS